Cinderella
& the CEO

MAUREEN CHILD

MILLS
BOON®
&
™

All the characters in this book have no existence outside the imagination of the author, and have no relation whatsoever to anyone bearing the same name or names. They are not even distantly inspired by any individual known or unknown to the author, and all the incidents are pure invention.

First published in Great Britain 2011
by Mills & Boon, an imprint of Harlequin (UK) Limited,
Large Print edition 2011
Eton House, 18-24 Paradise Road,
Richmond, Surrey TW9 1SR

© Maureen Child 2010

ISBN: 978 0 263 21706 3

Harlequin (UK) policy is to use papers that are natural, renewable and recyclable products and made from wood grown in sustainable forests. The logging and manufacturing process conform to the legal environmental regulations of the country of origin.

Printed and bound in Great Britain
by CPI Antony Rowe, Chippenham, Wiltshire

MAUREEN CHILD

is a California native who loves to travel. Every chance they get, she and her husband are taking off on another research trip. The author of more than sixty books, Maureen loves a happy ending and still swears that she has the best job in the world. She lives in Southern California with her husband, two children and a golden retriever with delusions of grandeur. Visit Maureen's website at www.maureenchild.com

To Kate Carlisle and Jennifer Lyon.
Thanks for all the e-mails
and phone calls and laughs.
You guys are the best.

One

"Hi, I'm your new housekeeper."

Tanner King looked the woman up and down, then once more, taking in her lush curves, heart shaped face and full lips. Late twenties, he guessed, she had long, blond hair tumbling around the shoulders of her yellow T-shirt and her faded jeans hugged her short, shapely legs like plastic wrap on a new CD. Her pale blue eyes sparkled and when she smiled, a dimple winked in her left cheek.

His body stirred and he shook his head, both

at her and at the completely physical response the woman engendered. "No, you're not."

"What?" She laughed and the sound of it rolled up and over him, sending blasts of heat through his body so fast, Tanner thought it had been way too long since he'd been with a woman.

He shook his head and said, "You're no house-keeper."

One of her blond eyebrows lifted. "And you know this because…"

"You're not old enough, for one."

"Well," she said, "as nice as that is, I can assure you I am old enough to clean a house. So who were you expecting? Mrs. Doubtfire?"

He instantly thought of that old comedy with the man dressed up like a fat old woman and nodded. "Yeah."

"Sorry to disappoint." She grinned at him and that single dimple of hers made another appearance.

Oh, she hadn't disappointed. That was the problem. There was nothing about this woman that was disappointing. Except for the fact that there was no way he was going to be able to hire her. He really didn't need the kind of distraction this woman so obviously was.

"Let's start over," she said, holding out her right hand. "My name's Ivy Holloway and you're Tanner King."

It was a long second or two before he shook her hand and quickly let her go again. He didn't much care for the buzz of something hot and sinful that had zipped up the length of his arm the moment he touched her. Which was proof enough to him that this was a bad idea.

Nothing had gone right since he had moved into what should have been a perfect house two months before. Why he was surprised at this latest setback, he couldn't say.

Sunset was spilling over the valley, twilight shifting slowly to night and the woman's soft, blond hair lifted with the cool breeze sliding off the mountain. She was watching him as if he were from Mars or something. And he supposed he couldn't blame her.

This is what happened when a man with a

penchant for privacy moved to a tiny town where everyone knew everything about everybody. He had no doubt that the town of Cabot Valley was curious about him. But he was in no hurry to satisfy that curiosity. He'd come here hoping to find some peace and quiet where he could work and be left the hell alone.

Of course, the peace and quiet thing had already disintegrated. He lifted his gaze to the borders of his property where acres of Christmas trees spread out as far as a man could see. It looked placid. Serene. And was anything but. Frustration simmered inside him briefly before he deliberately tamped it down again.

"Look," he said, moving to block the doorway by slapping one palm on the doorjamb, "I'm sorry you had to come out here, but you're not exactly what I was looking for. I'm happy to pay you for your time."

In Tanner's experience people—especially women—were always willing to be paid off. Former girlfriends received tasteful diamond bracelets and housekeepers who would clearly not work out could get a nice check. No harm. No foul.

"Why would you pay me when I haven't worked yet?"

"Because this is not a good idea."

"You don't need a housekeeper?" she asked, folding her arms beneath her breasts and at the same time lifting them high enough that he couldn't ignore them—not that he had been. Her breasts were round and full and the tops of them were just visible over the neckline of that T-shirt. Oh, he'd noticed.

"Of course I do."

"And your lawyer hired me for the job. What's the problem?"

The problem, he told himself, was that he hadn't been specific enough when his best friend and lawyer, Mitchell Tyler had offered to hire him a housekeeper. It was Tanner's own damn fault that he hadn't told the man to make sure the woman he hired was old and quiet and well past tempting.

Tanner was already behind on work thanks to

all the disruptions around here. He didn't need yet another distraction right under his nose all the time.

And Ivy Holloway would definitely be a distraction.

While he was lost in his own thoughts, the woman ducked beneath his arm and scooted into the house before he could stop her. There was no way to get her out again without just picking her up and carrying her. It wouldn't have been difficult. She was small enough that he could toss her over one shoulder and have her across the porch, down the steps and onto the lawn in a few seconds. But as if she knew just what he was considering, she walked further into the main room. Then she stopped and turned a slow circle, taking it all in.

"This place is amazing," she whispered and he followed her gaze.

Dark wood and glass made up most of the house, affording him a glorious view of the very Christmas tree lot that had become the bane of his existence in the last two months. The main room of the house was massive, dotted with oversized couches and chairs, grouped together in conversation knots that were never used. The hearth was river stone and was tall enough for Tanner to stand up in. Three-foot high bookcases ringed the room like a chair rail and gleaming tables sat atop warm, honey-colored oak floors. It was everything he'd wanted his house to be. Would have been perfect if not for—

"People have been dying to get a look at this house," she mused. "Ever since you bought the place and started your renovations, the town's been fascinated."

"I'm sure, but—"

"It's understandable," she added, throwing him a quick look. "After all, this place was empty for years before you bought it and it didn't look anything like *this*."

Oh, he knew that. Hadn't he paid a fortune to the King construction crews to spend ten months doing what should have taken two years? He'd known exactly what he wanted, and had one of his cousins, an architect, draw up the plans. Tanner had been meticulous. He'd built this place to be his sanctuary. His corner of the world, safe and inviolate.

He snorted derisively at how quickly his plans had fallen apart.

"Where's the kitchen?" she asked, interrupting his thoughts again.

He pointed. "Through there, but—"

Too late, she was already gone, her boot heels clacking merrily against the wood floor. Forced to follow her, Tanner did just that, managing to tear his gaze away from the curve of her butt only through sheer determination.

"Oh my God," she whispered as if she'd stepped into a cathedral.

The kitchen was huge, too. Bright, with its cream-colored walls and golden oak cabinets. Miles of granite countertop the color of honey topped dozens of cupboards and the big farmhouse sink overlooked a wide window with a view of the backyard. Even in twilight the yard was impressive, with sculpted trees and bushes and late summer flowers splashing the place with color.

"Cooking in here will feel like a vacation," she murmured, tossing him a quick smile. "You should see my kitchen. No counter space and a refrigerator that's older than I am."

She walked to the Subzero fridge and opened the door, cooing a little at all the space she found inside. Then she frowned and looked at him again. "Beer and salami? That's all you have in here?"

"There's some ham, too," he said a little defensively. "And eggs."

"Two."

"The freezer's full," he pointed out, though why he felt as though he had to explain himself to her was beyond him. "I'm not completely helpless."

She gave him a look usually reserved for particularly slow children. "This amazing kitchen and all you use is the microwave for frozen dinners?"

Tanner scowled. He'd been busy. Besides, he

was planning on cooking, or hiring someone to do it. Someday.

"Never mind." Shaking her head, she shut the refrigerator and said, "Okay, I'll pick up some groceries for you—"

"I can buy my own food."

"Oh," she assured him, "you're going to. But I'll do the ordering since that talent seems to have escaped you."

"Ms. Holloway." The two words sounded long-suffering, even to him.

"Oh," she waved a hand at him. "Call me Ivy. Everyone does."

"Ms. Holloway," he repeated deliberately and watched that one eyebrow lift again, "I already told you, your being here is not going to work."

"How do you know?" she asked, running the palm of one hand across the honey granite as if she were petting it. "I could be great. I might be the best housekeeper in the world. You could at least give me a try before you make up your mind."

Oh, he'd like to give her a try, Tanner thought. But not the way she meant. Her scent drifted to him from across the cooking island. She smelled of lemons and he caught himself before he could take a much deeper breath just to taste more of it.

If he had Mitchell here in front of him, Tanner thought he might just slug his old college room-mate dead in the face. For years, Mitchell and his wife Karen had been trying to get Tanner settled down with a 'nice' woman. They'd done the dinner party with a surprise guest thing. They'd thrown parties where they could parade a stream of women past him. All in an attempt to bring him out of his shell.

The problem was, he didn't think of his life as a shell. He'd spent plenty of years construct-ing the defenses around him and he didn't have the slightest interest in letting anyone else in. He had friends. He had his cousins and half brothers. He didn't need anyone else. But try telling that to your married friends. It was as if as soon as a man got married, he wanted every guy he knew in that boat with him. Mitchell was doomed to disappointment in Tanner's case. But damned if he didn't keep trying.

And Ivy Holloway was proof of that. Mitchell had probably taken one look at her and decided that the town beauty was one sure way to get Tanner involved in what was going on around him. It wasn't going to work.

"The thing is," he said before his body could talk his mind out of what he knew needed to be done, "I work at home during the night. I sleep during the day—or try to—" he muttered. With all the noise erupting around his bucolic retreat, sleep was getting tougher and tougher to manage. "So I can't have you making all kinds of noise while I'm working and—"

"What do you do?"

"What?"

"You said you work at home." She leaned her elbows on the countertop, propped her chin in her hands and asked, "What do you do?"

Her blue eyes were sharp and focused on him. "I design computer games."

"Really? Have you done any I would recognize?"

"I doubt it," he said, knowing full well that King games catered to young men more than women. "I don't design fashion or exercise games."

"Wow," she said softly. "That was patronizing."

Yeah, it had been. He hadn't expected her to call him on it, though. "It's just—"

"Try me," she said with a grin that had her dimple appearing again.

"Fine," he said, challenge in his voice. "The last game I designed was 'Dark Druids.'"

"Seriously?" Her eyes went wide. "That's great. I love that game. And, just so you know, I'm a ninth level Master Sage," she told him with a proud lift of her chin.

Instantly intrigued in spite of himself, Tanner gave her a considering look. He knew exactly how difficult his "Druid" game was and to reach the ninth level was impressive. "Really. How long did it take you?"

She shrugged and admitted, "Six months, but in my defense, I only played at night. So what are you working on now? Is it okay to ask, or is it a big secret?"

Six months? She'd scored that high in six months? He got e-mail letters from players complaining that he'd obviously made the game too hard as they'd only reached third level in more than a year of trying. He almost forgot that he was supposed to be getting rid of her. So she was more than beautiful. Smart, too. A deadly combination.

Still, Tanner had to stop himself from discussing his current game and the roadblock he'd hit the night before. If she was that good, maybe he could bounce a couple of ideas off her. He cut that thought off fast. He wasn't looking for a collaborator. In fact, she was keeping him from working. He was standing here talking to her when he should be upstairs buried in medieval magic—which proved his point that she was too much of a distraction.

"Secret, I guess," she said, clearly reading his expression. "Okay then, never mind. Why don't you go on and get to work and I'll take care of things around here?"

"I don't think—"

"You need a housekeeper," she told him flatly "and God knows, you desperately need someone to cook for you. And I need the extra money. I'll be so quiet, you'll never know I'm here. Promise. So why not just give me a chance?"

Clearly, she wouldn't leave without an argument and he didn't have time for one. It seemed easier at the moment to agree. "Fine. I'll be upstairs in the office. Third door on the left."

"Have fun!" She turned away and started opening cupboards, muttering to herself.

Tanner intended to talk to Mitchell and get him to fire the woman. Soon. She'd already forgotten he was there as she made notes on a tablet she'd found in a drawer. She was humming and the sound of it pushed him into moving. This wasn't going to work out. He'd give her tonight, but tomorrow, she'd have to go.

When he left the kitchen, she didn't even glance at him.

The minute she was alone, Ivy slumped against the beautiful kitchen countertop.

"That went well," she murmured to the empty room. She'd made him angry right off the bat. Though to be fair, she thought, he had already been angry when he opened the door to her. If she hadn't been so quick on her feet, she might not have gotten into the house.

And she'd had to get in. *Had* to have this job as housekeeper. Yes, the extra money would come in handy, what with everything she was trying to do at home right now, but that wasn't the real reason she was here—in enemy territory. That sounded odd, even to her. She had never actually had an enemy before. But she did now. A very rich, very powerful one.

But she wished she'd known ahead of time that her enemy was so gorgeous. One look at him and she'd actually had to lock her knees to keep them from buckling.

Tanner King should have a warning label slapped against his forehead. More than six feet of leanly packed muscle and long legs, the man was a walking hormone celebration. She knew because her own were still doing a happy dance that had her palms damp and her stomach doing twists and turns. From the moment he opened his front door, Ivy had felt as though she was trying to keep her feet during an earthquake.

His dark blue eyes, his thick black hair, shaggy and touching the collar of his shirt. His wide shoulders, narrow waist and his long legs all combined to make her insides quiver.

And that was something she hadn't counted on. How was she supposed to work for the man, subtly win him over, if her body was in a constant state of excitement?

"Maybe Pop was right," she muttered, remembering how her grandfather had tried to talk her out of this plan. Too late now though, she thought, stalking to the floor to ceiling cupboard on the far end of the room. As she'd hoped, it was a butler's pantry and one look inside at the mostly empty shelves told her that Tanner King was lucky he hadn't starved to death in the two months he had been living here.

Bur then it seemed that all he did was work on his computer games and make complaining phone calls to the sheriff.

About *her.*

She closed her eyes and took a deep breath before letting all the air slide from her lungs again. That's why she was here, of course. One too many visits from Sheriff Cooper who had told her only two days before that he didn't know how much longer he could placate Tanner King.

Closing the pantry doors, she leaned back against them and looked at the expansive room. Beautiful but empty. Sort of like its owner, she mused. What kind of man was it who could build a house this beautiful and leave it so bare?

"Well, that's what you're here to find out, isn't it, Ivy?" she told herself firmly.

She not only wanted to understand him, she wanted to make *him* understand her and this place he'd moved to. Before he ruined everything.

It wouldn't be easy, but Ivy didn't come from a family of quitters. Once her mind was made up, her grandfather often observed, it would take an act of God to change it. She was here and she wasn't going to leave until she'd helped Tanner King to see the light, so to speak.

A little nervous about this whole thing, she knew pretending to be nothing more than a part-time housekeeper was going to be hard. After all, she was a terrible liar. But then she didn't actually have to flat out *lie* either, did she? Ivy smiled to herself. It was more of a lie of omission and that wasn't really so bad, was it? If it was for the greater good?

"Man, I wonder how many people have consoled themselves with that particular thought."

She sighed a little, wishing things were different. But wishing didn't change a thing as she knew all too well. Besides, the game was in motion, she'd already made her first move, so there was nothing to do now but go forward. She was here. She'd do the job she came to do.

And one way or another, Tanner King would find out he'd met his match.

Two

"All I'm saying," Tanner King muttered darkly into the phone, "is that a man shouldn't have to be bothered by Christmas in the middle of August."

"Uh-huh." The voice on the other end of the line sounded amused. "Now you sound like those idiots who buy a house next door to an airport and then complain about the noise."

Tanner scowled out the window at the tree farm that bordered his one acre plot of land. At night, it looked deceptively peaceful. The scent of pine drifted to him on a soft breeze slipping beneath the partially opened window and he scowled. Looking at the place now, you'd never guess what a crowded, noisy place it was during the day.

"What's your point?"

"My point," his cousin said on a chuckle, "is that you knew that Christmas tree farm was there when you bought your place a year ago. No point whining about it now."

"A," Tanner told the other man, "I don't whine. And B, what kind of Christmas tree farm is open all year round? Nobody mentioned that when I bought this place."

Of course, he hadn't asked, either. But, Tanner thought in his own defense, who would? He'd bought his house more than a year ago and hadn't given his next-door neighbors much thought, beyond the fact that the trees made for a nice view from his windows. Christmas tree farms, by definition, were Christmas-based operations, right? At least that was how it was supposed to be. Shaking his head while his cousin's voice rang in his ear, Tanner again stared out the window of his office at the property next door.

He had moved in only two months ago—since the construction crew he'd hired right after buying the place had spent nearly ten months remodeling. When he'd finally settled in, he'd looked forward to some quiet. Who wouldn't have, with a tree farm as their closest neighbor? Instead though, he had spent the last two months watching a veritable parade of visitors to the Angel Christmas Tree farm.

Except for his neighbors, the house was everything he'd wanted. Glass and wood and surrounded by nearly an acre of land, he had all the privacy he required. Or so he'd thought. From the second story window, Tanner had quite a view. Acres of trees sprawled across the landscape, stretching out for what looked like miles. But then, it wasn't the trees themselves he was having a problem with. It was the farm owner's entrepreneurial spirit. Apparently the Angel family who owned the farm, had come up with the idea of expanding their holiday business into a year-round concern.

There were event weddings taking place nearly every weekend, hayrides, picnic sites and, God help him, even kids' birthday parties. All of which had resulted in a never ending stream of cars roaring up and down the narrow road in front of his property. The Angel tree farm was turning into a pain in his ass.

But that wasn't the worst part. No, the worst part was the music, piped out of speakers attached to telephone poles. Holiday music. In August. Blistering heat outside and Tanner was forced to listen to "White Christmas" on a daily basis.

While he was trying to sleep.

"You could consider giving up the whole 'live like a vampire' thing and sleep at night like most people," his cousin Nathan suggested.

"I tried that when I first got here," Tanner muttered, turning away from the view to stare at the flat screen computer monitor on his desk across the room. "You try working on a medieval war game while listening to the sound of 'Jingle Bells' in a never ending loop."

No, working at night had been the only reasonable solution, he thought, remembering the sexy woman roaming his house. How was he supposed to concentrate on work when he knew she was here? Right downstairs?

"Okay, forget I said that," Nathan told him. "I'd rather have you crabby as hell and that computer game you're working on finished by deadline. How's it coming, anyway?"

This was why his cousin had called in the first place. Tanner's company, King Games had entered into a partnership with Nathan's company, King Computers. The new computer game Tanner was designing would be included in the software of every new King PC. It was going to be huge. If Tanner finished the thing on time.

Which, thanks to the Angel tree farm—and now, Ivy Holloway—was looking less likely by the minute.

Of course, the game was actually near

completion. He'd done most of the art work months ago and the programmers had coded the damn thing. Now he was working out a few of the details in the graphics and story line itself and he was behind schedule. He could have handed the project off to any number of the designers who worked for him. But designing games was what Tanner enjoyed most—and this particular game was far too important to trust anyone else to do it the way he wanted it done.

Besides, a King game was damn well going to be designed by a King.

"I hit a snag last night," Tanner grumbled, scrubbing one hand across his eyes.

"We've got production set to roll in another month."

"Thanks, I've got a calendar. Don't need the reminder."

"I'm just saying, if we want the first of these games to be ready for the Christmas rush then you've got to bring it in on time." Nathan blew out a breath. "As it is, we'll be scrambling in production. We can't take a delay on this, Tanner."

"It'll be ready. Just don't talk to me about Christmas, okay?" Or about beautiful, clever blondes. He kept his mouth shut about Ivy. He didn't need to hear any teasing from his cousin on that score, too. Nathan was a legendary player. Had more women in his life than he could keep track of. If he got wind of what Mitchell had set Tanner up for this time, he'd never hear the end of it. Besides, she wouldn't be here long.

"Right. Look, I've got a meeting in fifteen minutes with the distributors. I'm going to be talking up this game and the new King PC so let's just stay on track here, okay?"

"Relax, Nathan. I know how important this is. To both of us."

His video/computer gaming company was already more successful than even he could have dreamed. Tanner had built his enterprise into a worldwide success—and this partnership with his cousin was going to put King Games into the stratosphere. Just where he wanted it.

All he had to do was focus.

And somehow, keep his mind off the woman downstairs.

Two hours later, groceries had been delivered from town and most of them were already stashed in the amazingly numerous cupboards.

Ivy was completely in love with Tanner King's house. *Especially,* she thought, *the kitchen.*

Oh, she loved her own place too, of course. The old Victorian where she'd grown up had plenty of character—lots of that character was grumpy, but still she loved it. There were memories etched into every square inch of the battered old house and she wouldn't trade it for anything. But if she were going to trade, she'd take Tanner King's house in a heartbeat.

"Honestly, the man has a kitchen to die for and he keeps it stocked with beer and pretzels. No wonder he needed help." She was talking to herself, which was understandable because the house was so quiet if she didn't, she might start feeling a little creeped out at the silence.

How he worked in such a barren atmosphere, she didn't know. And how he invented such intricate games that were filled with wit and magic while he was working in a black hole of solitude she'd never understand.

Ivy liked people. She thrived on the energy of being in the midst of things. Being a part of life. She was awake at dawn and resented having to close her eyes to sleep every night. There was just so much to do. So much to plan. So much to dream. She felt as though she never had enough time to accomplish everything she wanted to do.

Which made it even harder to understand a man like Tanner King choosing to shut himself away. Hard to imagine why anyone would want to live like that.

Two months Tanner King had been living in Cabot Valley and not a soul there knew him at all. Not even Merry Campbell who had been known to uncover a person's life story over a short cup of coffee. Of course, the man would have had to actually go into town and step into Merry's store for that to happen.

And he hadn't.

As far as Ivy knew, he hadn't been into town once since moving into this flawless, spectacular wood and glass palace. He had his few groceries delivered and avoided all other contact.

"Well," she corrected herself, "not all." He'd certainly been spending time talking to the sheriff of Cabot Valley. He'd lodged at least a dozen complaints about the Angel Christmas Tree Farm in the last couple of months. The crowds. The noise. The music. The traffic.

You'd think he'd have better things to do, she told herself firmly. But no, he'd moved into the valley and immediately tried to remake everything just the way he wanted it. Well, it wasn't going to work. They weren't going to change to suit Tanner King and the sooner she could make him see that, the better for all of them. But first, she had to make him like her. Become his friend. Introduce him around, maybe. Let him see that the Angel Christmas Tree Farm was a big part of the community.

And feeding him seemed like a good place to start.

Shaking her head, she opened the oven door, pulled out the fresh loaf of bread and set it on a cooling rack. While delectable scents filled the air, she turned to the stove and stirred the pot of soup. It smelled good despite being the ninety-minute quick start variety. Better than canned, but not as good as homemade. But at least he'd have fresh bread to go with it and she was fairly sure that this meal would be better than anything he'd made for himself in the last couple of months.

Her mom used to say that any man could be won over by a good meal and a warm smile.

She sure hoped Mom was right.

Because otherwise, Ivy would never be able to protect her Christmas tree farm from a rich man who wanted to shut it down.

Tanner couldn't work. He'd tried, but every time he entered the changes he wanted on the programming form, his mind drifted to the woman in his house. Blond hair. Blue eyes. Dimple. The sound of her breathy voice and the faint, lemony scent that clung to her. Damn it, it didn't seem to matter how many times he pushed thoughts of her from his head, she came right back a moment later.

And it was more than just mental images of her. How was a man supposed to keep his mind on work when he knew someone else was in the house? He hadn't heard a vacuum or anything, but she was no doubt wandering around with dust cloths or whatever. Poking into things. Looking around. Breathing his air.

"Damn it."

Tanner sat back in his desk chair and shoved both hands through his hair. Frustration tugged at the corners of his mind. He had thirty days to get the kinks worked out of this game. And he was wasting time sitting there thinking about Ivy Holloway.

"This is just not going to work," he muttered and reached for the phone.

After three rings, his lawyer picked up. "Hello?"

"Mitchell, you've got to fire that housekeeper."

The other man laughed shortly. "Hi, Tanner. Good to hear from you. Yeah, Karen's fine. Thanks for asking."

Tanner scrubbed one hand across his face. "Very funny. This isn't a social call."

"Yes, I picked up on that." Mitchell sighed. "The housekeeper hasn't even been there one full night and already you want her fired?"

Pushing up and out of his chair, Tanner stalked to the window and stared out at his nemesis, the tree farm. "I didn't want her in the first place, remember?"

A part-time housekeeper had sounded like a good idea in theory, two weeks ago when Mitchell had first suggested it. God knew he was tired of frozen or packaged dinners and doing his own damn laundry. But with the crunch to get the game done and his lack of sleep, now wasn't a good time.

"Forget it, Tanner. You need someone in there to cook and clean."

"Because more distraction is exactly what's required."

"You know," his old college roommate mused, "there's a fine line between brilliant recluse and nutcase hermit."

He frowned at the phone. "I'm not a hermit."

"Not yet." Sighing, his friend asked, "Would you rather she come in during the day while you're sleeping?"

"No." That would be all he needed, he told himself. Not only the noise from the tree farm, but someone inside his house making noise, too. Besides, he thought, remembering his sexy new housekeeper, if she were around when he was in bed, he'd be way too tempted to have her join him. No, better that she come in while he was working. At least then, he could tell her to stay away from wherever he happened to be and to clean around him.

"Then it's settled. Don't scare her off."

"I don't scare women," Tanner said, insulted at

the suggestion. And Ivy Holloway hadn't seemed the slightest bit intimidated by him. He wasn't sure if that was a good thing or a bad thing.

"My old friend, you scare everybody but me," Mitchell told him.

Scowling, Tanner thought about that for a second or two. He didn't like people much. Preferred his own company. Did that really make him a damn hermit? A scary one at that? When had that happened? When had he gone from being a private person to a solitary one?

Sighing heavily in resignation, he changed the subject.

"Mitchell, at least tell me there's something we can do about the damn tree farm."

He'd turned his lawyer onto the problem since Tanner's last conversation with the local Sheriff hadn't resolved a damn thing. Of course, that wasn't surprising. Naturally Sheriff Cooper would side with the local against a newcomer. Still though, something had to change.

His old friend said, "I've checked into it, and I can file an injunction, but it won't get you anywhere. That farm's been in the Angel family for three generations. The town's happy with it. Brings in plenty of tourist dollars and no local judge is going to side with you on this. You'll only stir things up and probably make them worse."

"How could it get worse?"

"Piss them off and maybe you'll have Christmas music playing all night, too," Mitchell grumbled. "Tanner, you've just got to find a way to work with them."

"Perfect," Tanner muttered, sitting down behind his desk. He had the house he'd always wanted and it was sitting next to a torture factory. "You know, it's not just the traffic and the damn noise, Mitchell. I've got kids wandering over here from that farm and climbing my trees. That's a liability nightmare waiting to happen. Not to mention the fact that I don't own a dog, yet I *do* now own a pooper scooper of all damn things."

He wasn't sure, but he thought he heard Mitchell laugh.

"It's not funny. Do you know there's an event wedding over there nearly every weekend? And last weekend, there were at least thirty little kids running and screaming all over the place."

"Yeah see, that's the problem," Mitchell told him. "You go into court complaining about children making happy noises at a Christmas tree farm and you look like the ultimate Scrooge. And that's not going to make you real popular around there. It's a small town, Tanner. You knew that when you moved there. Cabot Valley is nothing like L.A."

"No kidding." Actually, the size of the tiny town was one of the things that had drawn Tanner to this part of Northern California. Cabot Valley was only a couple of hours by car away from Sacramento on one side and Lake Tahoe on the other. He could have city when he needed it, but he could be left the hell alone otherwise.

He hadn't even been into town since he moved in. He ordered groceries from the store and had them delivered. When he did leave the house, he didn't bother buying gas in Cabot Valley because he didn't want the locals getting used to seeing him around. He didn't want to be drawn into conversations that could lead to people dropping by his house just to be neighborly. He wasn't looking to make friends. He just wanted to be left alone to do his work in peace.

At least, that had been the plan.

So far, that wasn't happening.

"All I'm saying is give it a while," Mitchell told him. "Settle in. See if you can't find a way to work around this problem before you start making enemies."

Scowling, Tanner silently admitted he didn't want enemies any more than he wanted to make friends. He just wanted some damn peace and quiet.

"Fine," he snapped. "But tell me this. You won't get rid of the housekeeper and you can't do anything about the damn tree farm. Why is it haven't I fired you?"

"Because I'm the only person you know who'll

tell you the truth whether you want to hear it or not."

"Good point. I'm hanging up now."

"So am I. And Tanner…be nice."

He hit the off button and frowned. Even irritated, Tanner could admit that Mitchell was right. He did appreciate the truth. Heaven knew he'd been lied to enough as a kid to last him a lifetime. His mother always had a ready story handy to explain why she couldn't be at his school for a meeting or why she had to leave him with the housekeeper for a month or two while she flew off to Gstaad or Florence or wherever her latest lover had lived.

Instantly, he pushed those old memories away. He wasn't a kid anymore and his childhood had nothing to do with the here and now. The point was, Mitchell was right. And outside of his family—innumerable cousins and half brothers—there were very few people Tanner trusted. Mitchell was one of them.

As he set the phone down, he leaned back, closed his eyes and just for a moment, reveled in the quiet. No Christmas songs. No cars racing along the road. No kids shrieking in his front yard.

No sound from downstairs, either. *What was she doing down there? What kind of house-keeper was that quiet?* Quietly, he went downstairs, and stopped just outside the kitchen door. Something smelled incredible and his stomach grumbled in anticipation. Tanner was so used to just nuking a frozen dinner in the microwave—it had been a long time since he'd actually been *hungry.* Hard to find appreciation for flash frozen pot pies or Salisbury steaks.

He pushed the door open and stood silently in the doorway. There were mixing bowls in the sink, water gushing into them and flour was scattered across the counter making it look as if it had snowed in there. A cupboard door was hanging open, and a bowl full of fruit was on the counter. His gaze shifted to where his new housekeeper was dancing over to the table and setting two places while humming—off-key—and he sighed when he recognized "The Little

Drummer Boy." *Another Christmas song. Was this whole town nuts for Christmas?* Shaking his head, he walked to the sink and shut the water off.

Instantly, she spun around, hand clapped to her chest. In the next second, Ivy shot him a near blinding smile.

"Wow. You move quietly. Scared me. Next time ring a bell or something, okay?"

"If you'd remember to turn off the water, you would have heard me."

One of her eyebrows lifted. "I would have shut it off. I'm soaking the bowls."

He ignored that, reached over and closed the cupboard door. "I thought you were here to clean. The kitchen looks like a bomb went off in here."

She just looked at him. "Has anyone ever told you that you're wound a little tight?"

"Just recently, actually."

"Not surprised," she said, then shrugged. "But that's okay."

"Thanks so much."

"No problem. We've all got our quirks." She turned away, grabbed a dishcloth and swiped up the spilled flour. "And as to the mess in here, I was busy. Besides, you have to actually make something dirty before you can clean it."

"Mission accomplished," he said wryly, then sniffed the air. "Though whatever you've been doing smells good."

She smiled slowly and the curve of her mouth tickled that dimple into life in her cheek. A buzz quickened inside Tanner and he had to battle it into submission.

"I guess it would, after living on frozen dinners for two months," she said. Walking to the stove, she swept a spoon through a pot of something that smelled delicious. His stomach rumbled in appreciation.

"What is that?"

"Soup."

The soup he made never smelled that good, he thought and told himself that maybe this hadn't been such a bad idea after all. She seemed to be good at the job and in her defense, he really hadn't heard her down here at all. Still, he hadn't been able to concentrate just knowing she was in the house.

Then his stomach made its opinion clear again and he wondered if there wasn't some way they could make this work. "We really haven't talked about this job," he said.

"Except for the fact that you don't want me here, no," she agreed, smiling.

Did she smile over everything? he wondered, then shook that thought away as irrelevant. "I admit, having someone in the house while I'm working is problematic. I like it quiet."

"Yeah, I guessed that much." She turned to a cupboard, got down two bowls and set them on the counter. "Personally, I don't know how you can stand it. Too much quiet can make you crazy."

"I wouldn't know," he said dryly, thinking of all the interruptions he'd put up with since moving to the supposedly quiet countryside.

She glanced at him and grinned. "Was that sarcasm?"

"I believe so," he admitted, leaning one shoulder against the doorjamb.

"I like it," she said moving to the cooking island to pop a fresh loaf of bread out of its pan and onto a rack. "Proves you do have a sense of humor. So what do you want to talk about?"

"Expectations," he said. "I need quiet to work. But I suppose I do need a housekeeper, too. What we need to do is work out a timetable that's acceptable to both of us."

"Seems reasonable," she mused and walked to the cooking island.

His gaze followed her. "You made bread?"

"Yeah." She shrugged. "It's nothing special. Just quick bread. I mean, I didn't have time to let yeast rise and everything, but this is good, trust me."

He studied her as she moved comfortably around the big room. She'd baked bread and if he wasn't mistaken that was homemade soup on the stove. She'd been in the house for two hours and somehow she'd already taken over. How was it possible? And was it that important, his mind taunted as he savored the scents filling the brightly lit kitchen.

Wouldn't hurt, he told himself, *to eat what she'd prepared.* Then they'd talk about this and find a way for her to be here while not bothering him. He wasn't a damn hermit, he told himself. He was a busy man with no time for interruptions. There was a difference. He preferred order to chaos, that was all.

There were rules that Tanner lived by. Simple. Uncomplicated. He kept to himself. He trusted his brothers and cousins. And most importantly, he avoided relationships that lasted more than a week or two. When he wanted a woman, he went out and found someone looking for nothing more than he was—a couple of weeks of pleasure and a quick goodbye.

Ivy Holloway was definitely not that kind of woman.

So there was no reason for him to allow her to stay, was there?

Three

"Well," she asked. "You hungry?"

"Yeah," he said, tearing his gaze from her pale blue eyes. "I am."

"I'll join you if that's okay," she said, motioning for him to take a seat at the pedestal table set into the curve of the bay window. "I didn't have a chance to eat before I left home."

"Where is home?"

There was a long pause before she said, "Um, here. Cabot Valley." She filled the bowls at the stove, then carried them to the table.

The scent of the soup wafted up to him and

Tanner breathed deep, reaching for his napkin and soupspoon. "I guessed that much," he said dryly. "I meant, do you live close by?"

"Sure." She slipped a bread knife from a drawer and cut two thick slices of fresh bread. Lightly buttering them, she carried them to the table and offered him one. Then she sat down opposite him and added, "You know what they say. In a small town, nothing's far from anything."

He frowned at her evasion, but let it go. Frankly, his stomach was demanding more attention at the moment, so he gave in and sampled her soup. Good. Very good. He'd eaten half the bowl before he knew what was happening and then glanced up to see her smiling at him.

"What's so funny?"

"Not funny," she told him. "Is it so wrong for a cook to enjoy watching someone appreciate what she made?"

"No," he said with a shrug. "I suppose not. And the bread's good, too, but you do know you can buy this stuff now. Packaged and sliced."

She frowned at him. "And is it as good as this bread?"

"No, but it's easier."

"Easier isn't always better."

"Actually, I agree with you on that," he admitted, looking into her eyes. *She was more,* he reminded himself, *than just a gorgeous woman with a body to make a grown man weep.* Which, as he'd already warned himself, wasn't necessarily a good thing. Smart, sexy women could bring an unwary man down faster than anything else.

"Look at that," she told him. "We're practically friends already!"

"I wouldn't go that far," he said, finishing his soup. Before he could get up to refill his bowl, she was already standing and walking to the stove.

"You don't have to wait on me," he said.

"Trust me," she answered. "If I *had* to, I probably wouldn't. But consider it part of my job, okay? Housekeepers generally take care of more than the house, don't they? I mean," she continued as she carried the bowl back and set it down in front of him. "I've never been a housekeeper before, but seems to me that the job also includes taking care of the house owner."

He shook his head. "I don't need taking care of, thanks. Been doing just fine on my own most of my life."

"No family then?"

"Why would you say that?"

She pulled off a piece of her bread and popped it into her mouth. "Just that, if you've got family, you're not really on your own, are you?"

"That would depend on the family, wouldn't it?"

"Good point." She sat back in her chair and studied him until Tanner frowned.

"What?"

"Nothing, just wondering about why you don't like your family."

"I didn't say that."

"Sure you did."

"Are you always this direct?" He set his spoon down and leaned back in his chair. Folding his arms across his chest, he assumed an instinctive defensive posture.

"I try to be," she said. "No point in playing games, is there? Then you never get to know people because everyone's too busy pretending to be something they're not. Easier all the way around to be up front and…"

Her voice trailed off and Tanner said, "Well don't stop now, you're on a roll."

Ivy shook her head. "Never mind."

Uncomfortable now, because she *was* playing a game that she wished she weren't, Ivy changed the subject. Leaning her forearms on the table she said, "Why don't we talk about the job instead. What you want. What you don't want. Then we'll work from there."

"Okay." He nodded, thought for a moment and said, "What I want is quiet. Something that seems to be damned hard to come by around here."

She stiffened a little, stung and unable to show it. "I don't know," she said offhandedly, "Cabot Valley's really a very quiet place."

"Maybe the town is, but Christmas central here is a different story."

"You have something against Christmas?"

"In August, yeah."

She bit her tongue to keep the sharp retort she wanted to give him locked inside. Instead, she only said, "A year-round Christmas spirit seems like a good idea to me. People are always friendlier during the season. Kinder, somehow."

He laughed shortly, a harsh sound with no humor in it. "Oh yeah, retailers are notoriously kinder at Christmas."

"I'm talking about people. In general."

"The ones who spend themselves into bankruptcy and then have nervous breakdowns because nothing turned out the way they thought it would? Or how about the kids waiting for a Santa that never shows up? Or the drunks killing people on the road?" He snorted again. "Yeah, that's the kind of thing we should see all year."

"Isn't Christmas huge for your business?"

"I just build the games. I don't force people to buy them."

"Wow." Ivy looked at the dark, fierce expression on his face and knew that this was going to be much harder than she'd thought. Not only did Tanner King want to be isolated and alone, he actually *hated* Christmas. She'd never met anyone who hated the holiday before and she wasn't sure what to say to him now. How did you argue with someone who was determined to see only the negative in a situation?

And why, she couldn't help wondering, *did he feel that way?*

As if reading her expression clearly, he muttered, "Sorry. Didn't mean to go off like that."

"It's okay," she said, watching as the shutters over his eyes closed again, sealing him in and her out. He'd taken a mental step back and did it so neatly she knew it was a way of life for him. "But I have to ask, if you hate Christmas so much, why'd you buy a house right next door to a Christmas tree farm?"

He shot a glance out the window at the

darkness, and as if he could see the farm, shook his head. "Because I thought it would be quiet. I thought that Christmas would be the only time I would be bothered by it." He shifted his gaze back to hers. "Turns out, the owner of the farm feels the same way you do. Year-round Christmas is the theme."

"Is it really so bad?"

"Yeah." He picked up his bowl and spoon, then carried them to the sink. Setting them down in the mixing bowl full of water, he turned. Bracing his hands on the counter behind him, he said, "I've got kids running in and out of my yard, a dog I've never seen leaving messes for me to clean up and holiday music blaring all day long. It's that bad."

"Have you tried talking to the owners?" she asked, knowing damn well he hadn't. If he had once come to her, she might have tried to accommodate him. She wasn't sure how, but she'd have tried. Instead, he'd gone to the sheriff, setting himself up as her enemy and leaving her no other choice but to fight this stealth war.

"No. I spoke to the sheriff. Several times. But haven't had any luck with it yet."

"You know, Angel trees has been in this valley—"

"—for more than a hundred years," he finished for her. "Yes, I've heard. That doesn't mean they have the right to make their neighbors miserable. I'm guessing the Christmas carols they assault me with every damn day aren't heard wherever you live."

She winced, but hid it as best she could. Who hated Christmas carols?

"I don't think it's ever been a problem before. I mean," she said, "the person who used to own this property, Mrs. Mansfield, she loved Christmas. She used to work at the farm during the season, selling jams and jellies and the wreaths she made."

And she'd been like a surrogate grandmother to Ivy. Just remembering the old woman made Ivy's heart ache at her loss. If she'd known when Mrs. Mansfield died that a modern day Scrooge would be buying her property, Ivy would have mourned her loss even harder. But the deed was done and Tanner King was the new owner and she somehow had to get through to him. Although that task was looking more and more difficult every second.

"Maybe if you found a way to work with them…"

"The only thing people understand is money and power," he told her flatly, crossing his arms over his broad chest again.

"That's not true of everyone."

He smirked at that, but didn't argue the point. Instead, he said, "We were going to talk about the job."

"Right. Okay then, what is it you want from me?" The instant the words came out of her mouth, Ivy wanted to call them back. She'd sounded a little more seductive than she'd intended.

His eyes narrowed briefly, then, as if he were deliberately mentally moving on, he said, "How long will it take you to clean and make a meal for me every day?"

She had to think about it. Big house. Lots of rooms. Still, it wasn't as if he were a partier. Everything she'd seen so far had been organized to the point that the beautiful house was more like a model home than a real one. She half expected to see a realtor pop out of a closet, talking about staging.

"A couple of hours a day, probably," she said, knowing that would be stretching it. She could probably clean the whole house in a half hour considering how barren it was. The cooking was different of course, but still doable.

"All right then." He nodded. "Then we'll try it for a week. See how it goes."

A week wasn't very long, she thought. But she would be *here*. On his turf. She could wear him down inside a week, she told herself. Wasn't her grandfather always saying that nobody could take a stand against Ivy Holloway and come out the winner?

Well, she was going to put that theory to the test this week.

And she couldn't afford to lose.

* * *

"I still say this is a bad idea." Mike Angel's voice sounded like sandpaper on stone and his deeply tanned, weathered face folded into lines of disapproval.

Ivy sighed, knowing her grandfather was not going to stop trying to argue her out of her plan. From the moment she got home from Tanner's house an hour ago, Mike had been muttering and grumbling. "Pop, we've already talked about this."

"I talked," he countered. "You're not listening."

"I did, too," she told him. "And I made my own decision. Just like you taught me to do. Remember?"

His scowl only deepened. "Hardly fair play throwing my own words back at me."

Ivy smiled at him. Her grandfather had always been there for her. He'd been a constant in her life since the first week she and her mother had moved in with him following Ivy's father's death. She was ten that year and the older man had stepped into the void left by Tony Holloway and had become both father and grandfather to Ivy. She had spent countless hours walking the acreage of the tree farm at his side. She'd learned early where to plant, when to plant and when to cut. She'd worked alongside him and his employees to trim the pines into Christmas tree shape and along the way she'd become as much a part of the land as Mike was.

Which was exactly why he'd felt comfortable retiring to Florida to join his daughter while leaving the tree farm in Ivy's hands.

The only problem was, Mike was having a bit of trouble letting go. Especially with the problem of Tanner King hanging over their heads.

"The man's been trying to shut us down for the last two months, Ivy." Mike settled deeper into his worn, brown leather chair. "I don't see how you going to work for him is going to make the situation any better."

Ivy grinned at the older man. "To quote my grandfather… 'Am I not destroying my enemies when I make friends of them?'"

Mike snorted and shook his head until his flyaway gray hair nearly did fly away. "That's Abraham Lincoln, not me."

"Yes, but you're the one who always said it to me."

"So I'm supposed to feel better that at some point you actually *did* listen to me?"

"Exactly!" Ivy crossed the room, sat down on the brown leather ottoman in front of him and placed her hands on his knees. "You said you trusted me to take care of the farm. To protect the Angel family legacy. Did you mean it?"

His mouth worked furiously as he sucked in a gulp of air. "Course I meant it, but that doesn't—"

"So that means you trust me to make the right decisions for us, right?"

"Yeah, but—"

"Pop…either you trust me or you don't. So which is it?"

"You know all the right words to use when it suits you, don't you Ivy?" He reached out, patted her cheek and sighed. "Just like your mother,

God help me. Never could win an argument with her, either."

While Mike went on to complain a bit more, Ivy took a minute to simply enjoy the sound of his voice. In a few days, he'd be on a flight headed for Florida. Even if she had to tie him into his seat.

"I don't feel right about leaving here," Mike said, his voice a low grumble. "Seems to me until this gets straightened out, I ought to be here. Backing you up. In case you need help."

Though she loved him to pieces for wanting to stay, Ivy was just as set on his leaving. Oh, she was going to miss him desperately, she knew. But sometimes change was a good thing. And it would be for the beloved grandfather whose arthritis was bothered more every winter on the mountain. Besides, Ivy's mom really needed him.

Her mom had moved to Florida two years before and now she wanted her father—Mike, to move out there with her. He had been excited about the move, too. Until Tanner King had started making trouble for them. Her grand-father was too much of a mother hen to want to leave.

"Pop, you know as well as I do that Mom needs you. She's started that nursery and you're the plant guy in the family."

He rubbed his cheek with a work worn hand. "You need me, too, Ivy. Going up against a King isn't going to be easy. That family's practically royalty in California. If he goes to a judge, he might shut you down. Then where will you be?"

"Fighting him in court, if I have to," Ivy said, wincing at the very thought of it. She couldn't afford a court case. Heck, she probably couldn't afford to hire a lawyer at this point. She had every spare dime invested in the tree farm. Not to mention the loan she'd taken out to finance her dreams.

She had such plans for the place. And some of them were already working out. For the last few months, they'd been hosting weddings at the farm and had made such a name for themselves that they were getting couples from as far away as Los Angeles and Seattle. With the acres of trees, a wildflower strewn meadow boasting a fast-moving stream, Angel Weddings was fast becoming one of the hottest spots for a romantic setting in the state.

Then there were the birthday parties.

She cringed a little, remembering Tanner's grumbling about the kids running from her property to his. But in her defense, it wasn't always easy corralling fifteen or twenty kids. A few of them might have strayed onto his yard, but mostly, they were content to play in the bounce house. Or to help feed the animals Angel Farm kept in a small petting zoo. Hmm. She was willing to bet that Tanner didn't know about the pygmy goats or he'd have been complaining about them as well.

But the thing she was most proud of was her new Adopt-a-Tree program.

People could choose their Christmas tree months in advance and then come whenever they wanted to, to help care for the tree, water it, shearing. Kids learned how trees grew and how important the environment was to everyone and their parents enjoyed spending time with their kids.

Adopting a tree stretched out the Christmas season and to Ivy's way of thinking, kept families wrapped in that lovely spirit all year. And, while the people were at Angel Christmas Tree Farm, they usually had lunch at the newly established café and bought decorative items and crafts made by the ladies in town at the gift store.

She was turning their family business around *and* helping the local economy. She was so close to making Angel Christmas Tree Farm a year-round financial success. At least, she would be, if she had the chance. But if Tanner King did end up hiring a lawyer, all of her plans would drain away. She might even end up losing the home she loved so much to pay for lawyers she couldn't afford.

"It'd be different if only David hadn't—"

Her grandfather's words ended abruptly, but

it wasn't soon enough to keep an old familiar ache from settling around Ivy's heart. David. The man she had been about to marry four years ago. Until the car accident that had killed him instantly.

"I didn't mean to bring it up," Mike said quickly. "But damn it, if David were here, it'd be different. I could leave knowing you were safe."

She forced a laugh she knew he needed to hear. "Pop, I'm perfectly safe here and you know it. I'm not some fragile flower in a hothouse. I'm a tree farmer and most of the people who work here helped to raise me."

"It's not the same."

"No," she said wistfully. "it's not. But David's gone."

She'd mourned his loss for a long time, but as her grandfather reminded her, you couldn't bury yourself along with your heart. You had to move on and keep going.

Besides, it wasn't as if she would be really alone when Mike moved, anyway.

Not with ten part-time employees, people constantly running in and out of her house and an entire small town far too interested in her life. Still, she thought as she watched her grandfather worry, it was going to be hard, not having her family with her every day.

All too soon, she'd come home to an empty house, with only the memories of laughter and arguments and conversations to keep her company. Her gaze swept the familiar front room, lightly touching on the books haphazardly stacked in bookshelves and piled on tables. The handmade quilt her late grandmother had fashioned draped across the back of the sofa. The stone fireplace Mike had built when he and Grandma had first taken over the Angel family home. Scarred wooden floors, pale peach walls and the scent, as always, of evergreens.

Ivy's heart was in this old house. In this farm. In every tree on her acreage. And she would do whatever she had to do to protect every last seedling out there.

"At least tell me how you think working for

this guy is going to help the situation any," Mike said, catching her attention.

"It was actually Mr. King's lawyer's idea," she said and continued despite Mike's snort of derision. Everyone in the county knew how Mike Angel felt about lawyers. "Mitchell Tyler is his name and he was very nice when he called last week. You know, right after Sheriff Cooper came out to see us about the latest complaint?"

"I remember."

And judging by the look in his eye, the memory only fueled the flames of his anger. Being told by the local sheriff that the new guy in town was out to get you was not something anyone wanted to hear.

"Anyway," she said, trying to distract her grandfather from his anger, "Mitchell explained that he needed to hire Tanner a housekeeper and that he thought it would be a great way for me to convince Tanner that I'm not his enemy. He thinks that if we just get to know each other that Tanner might be more willing to listen to reason."

"Tanner." Mike snorted. "What kind of name is that, anyway? And Mitchell. Who names these people?"

"I like the name Tanner," she said. "It's masculine and strong and—" She broke off when she caught her grandfather's raised eyebrows.

She sighed. "The point is, Mitchell's trying to talk Tanner into relaxing and to stop making the complaints. But he says if I can worm my way into his good graces that could help the situation."

"And how did he hear about you? This Mitchell, I mean."

"Remember, I met him several months ago when he was up here delivering building permits and things for the crew that redid Mrs. Mansfield's house for Tanner."

"Harriet Mansfield. Now that was a good neigh-bor."

"Yes, but she's gone and Tanner's there now. We have to make him like it here, Pop, or he's going to make trouble for us."

"Like to see him try it," her grandfather muttered.

"Well I *don't* want to see him try it," Ivy said, leaning forward until she could meet her grandfather's steely blue eyes with her own. "He's rich and powerful and crabby. Not a good combination to have in an enemy."

"And you're gonna turn him around, are you?"

"I'm going to try," Ivy told him.

"If you fail?"

"I won't," she insisted. "Tanner's not a bad guy, Pop. He's just too…closed up. I'm going to open up his world for him."

Her grandfather's eyes narrowed on her thoughtfully. "You're not thinking of maybe…"

"Maybe what?"

"*You* know. You're young and pretty. He's young and rich."

"*POP!*"

"Wouldn't be the first time a woman's head was turned by a rich, powerful man."

"I don't care about his money. And I'm not

looking for romance." She shook her head. "I already had my shot at true love."

Her grandfather chuckled. "You really are young, Ivy, if that's what you think. You loved David, I know. But it won't be the last time you love, I sincerely hope. There'll be someone else for you along the road. Just don't look for it where you'll only find disappointment."

She flushed a little, remembering that swamping sensation of heat she'd felt at first sight of Tanner King. How just looking into his eyes made her stomach swim and her knees go weak. How the sound of his voice had seemed to shiver along her nerve endings.

But Mike was right, she told herself. Being Tanner's friend, introducing him to life in a small town and with any luck getting him to be less of a Scrooge was one thing. Romance was something else entirely. Men like him didn't go for women like her. And if they did, it wasn't a long-term commitment they were thinking about.

"I promise," she said softly. "I'm not looking for anything from Tanner except a cease-fire."

Mike studied her for a long minute, then patted her cheek again. "Well then, I say Tanner King doesn't stand a chance. Once Ivy Angel Holloway gets going, there's not a power on earth to stop her."

Four

The next morning, Ivy and Mike were in Cabot Valley Bank to talk about the balloon payment due on the loan she had taken out. She was as nervous as a child at the dentist waiting to get a cavity filled.

While she and her grandfather sat quietly, the bank manager, Steve Johnson, looked over their loan papers with a slow shake of his head. Finally, he looked up and met her gaze.

"Thanks for coming in, Ivy," he said. "I just wanted the three of us to have a sit-down to talk about the due date on this loan."

"Trust me when I say that I know the payment is almost due," she told him and was grateful when Mike reached over and gave her hand a pat. "It's not going to be a problem."

She sincerely hoped.

Ivy had taken out a big loan to improve and expand the farm, and she'd gotten a terrific interest rate—because she'd agreed to a huge balloon payment that would come due all too soon. If she didn't pay up, she could lose everything. The moment that thought entered her mind, she shoved it away and buried it. No room for bad karmic thoughts, she told herself.

Besides, as long as the big wedding they had scheduled came off without a hitch, there wouldn't be a problem.

"Steve," Mike said softly, "I've known you since you were a kid sneaking onto the farm at night to play hide-and-seek with your pals."

Steve squirmed uneasily in his chair. "That's—

"My point is," Mike said, "you know the Angel

family well enough to know we never fail to pay our debts."

"Of course I know that," Steve answered.

"Good." Ivy interrupted before either man could speak again. She appreciated her grandfather's support, but she was the one who'd taken out the loan It was her responsibility to pay it off. "I'll see you in a couple of weeks to make that payment, Steve. You can count on it."

When she stood up, so did the bank manager. He held out one hand across his desk and Ivy took it in hers. Mike nodded at him, and as they left, Steve said, "You know I only wish you the best, Ivy."

"I know that," she assured him and didn't speak again until she and Mike were in the main room of the bank.

The old building shone like a well cared for jewel. Wood walls were polished and the windows and floor gleamed from careful cleaning. Three or four people were lined up waiting for the tellers. Even a whisper carried in the room, since the high ceilings acted like an echo chamber or something. So Ivy was very quiet as she told her grandfather, "Don't worry, I know what I'm doing."

He slung one arm around her shoulder and steered her toward the front door. "I know you do, Ivy girl. I just want it all to go well, is all."

"It will. I promise."

As they stepped outside, Ivy took a deep breath and made a solemn, silent vow. She would make the balloon payment, then finish paying off the loan. She'd keep her farm, her family's legacy and once this loan was paid off, she'd never again take such a high-risk gamble.

Three days later, Tanner was no closer to solving the problems with the game. He blamed it on Ivy, of course. The woman was everywhere. And even when she wasn't actually *in* the house, her scent lingered, the thoughtful touches she'd left in her wake remained.

The fresh flowers she brought in and arranged in vases and pitchers to leave all over the house. The sandwiches she made and left wrapped for him in the refrigerator. The fresh fruit that he'd become accustomed to snacking on when he wandered through the empty rooms searching for inspiration.

Everywhere he looked, Ivy was there.

He should be trying to find a way to get rid of her, he knew. Instead, he'd spent most of his time wondering when she would be back. A dangerous situation but one he didn't seem to be able to avoid. Thoughts of her stayed with him long after she was gone.

Even the Christmas tree farm seemed different lately. He'd noticed that the volume on the damn carols had been cut way back—a fact for which he was grateful. Now the incessant music was no more than a background hum of irritation rather than the overpowering aggravation he was used to. Though he was curious as to why they were suddenly being so accommodating.

He looked out the window at the tree farm and the late afternoon sun speared into his eyes. That was another thing. He'd been waking up earlier since Ivy had been coming around. The only explanation he could come up with for the switch in his sleeping pattern was that his dreams were so full of her, his subconscious was waking him early so that he had more time with her.

Not that he was making use of that extra time. No, he was determined to keep his distance from the woman. She was clever and funny and sexy enough to make him want to grab hold of her every time she entered a room. But the fact was, he wasn't going to risk a brief fling with a woman who had *permanent* practically stenciled on her forehead.

Ivy was white picket fences and children at her knee.

Tanner was a solitary man and he liked it that way.

Never the twain would meet.

"Great. Now you're getting poetic." He turned from the window, walked to his desk and sat down. Glaring at the computer screen where his muscle-bound warrior knight stood glaring back at him, Tanner muttered, "Work. Damn it, keep your mind on the damn game and get it done."

This was the solution that had seen him through his life. As soon as he was old enough, Tanner had laid out a pattern for how he wanted his life to be. Orderly. Might seem boring to others, but for him, there was peace in rules. His childhood had been barely restrained chaos with a mother who drifted from one adventure to the next, always dragging her reluctant son behind her.

He'd long ago decided that his life would be different. It would be steady. Controlled. Organized. There was no room for chaos when structure ruled the situation. And his main rule was that when it was time for work, nothing else intruded.

Tanner had never had trouble with that self-imposed imperative until Ivy Holloway had come into his life. Now, he was forced to struggle to keep his mind on what used to be the most important thing in his life. His company. His designs. His future.

Shaking his head, he picked up a pen and tapped it against the sketch pad in front of him. He focused on the image of the knight on his computer screen, standing in a barren field of rocks and dead grass, the body of an evil troll at his feet.

"If the knight uses the enchanted sword against the troll, then there has to be a consequence," Tanner muttered, glaring at the knight as if this problem were all the character's fault.

When the truth was, Tanner's focus was still shattered. It seemed thoughts of Ivy were never far away no matter how much he fought them. Hell, how could he keep his mind on the problems faced by his game's hero when he knew Ivy Holloway was just downstairs?

He shoved one hand through his hair. One woman shouldn't have this kind of effect on a man. For God's sake, less than a week ago, he hadn't even known she existed.

Gritting his teeth, Tanner told himself that he might finally end up firing Mitchell over this all too alluring housekeeper.

"Troll," he muttered. "Keep your mind on the damn dead troll."

"I'm guessing there aren't many people in the world who get to say that during an ordinary work day."

He spun around to face the bane of his recent existence. She stood in the open doorway to his office, one hand resting lightly atop a vacuum cleaner. Her jeans were faded and her dark red T-shirt clung to her breasts and narrow waist in a way that made a man want to define those curves with his own hands. She was a temptation, pure and simple. And he was losing the battle to stay indifferent.

"I didn't hear you come up."

She grinned and that dimple he so looked forward to seeing appeared in her cheek. "That was the deal, remember? Quiet as a mouse. Not disturbing you."

"Right. Yeah, I know." He frowned at the vacuum. "Judging by that, you're about to disturb me though, right?"

She patted the upright, pale blue appliance.

"I sure am. So I thought I'd warn you first. Tell you to close your door against the noise."

"Fine," he acknowledged. "Not like I'm making any progress here anyway."

"Bad day at the joust?" she quipped.

"You could say that," Tanner admitted. "My knight has vanquished his foe far too easily."

She straightened up and curiosity flared in her eyes. "So what do you do about it?"

"That's the question. If the game's too easy, people complain. If it's too hard, people complain. So I walk a fine line. Right now, the game's leaning toward easy. Gotta come up with a fix." He stared into her eyes, caught up in the excitement he saw gleaming there. How long had it been since he'd been really *excited* about anything? "The question is," he said, "should it be a magical consequence or something a little more human?"

He shouldn't be asking her opinion, he told himself sternly. The games were his domain and he rarely listened to anyone else's input. The fact that she was standing there in the doorway, intruding on his work time was his own damn fault though, for leaving the door open in the first place. But then again, maybe he'd been hoping for an interruption.

Hard as it was to admit, Tanner thought, in the last few days that Ivy had been coming to his house every afternoon, he'd become accustomed to her. More than that, he'd actually begun looking forward to seeing her. So much so that he was shifting slowly out of his vampire work schedule.

So what did that say?

"What do you think?" he asked, not really expecting her to solve his problem, but not ready to stop talking to her or looking at her, either.

She abandoned the vacuum, stepped into the room and glanced at the walls where framed posters of his more popular games were hung. Silently admiring them with a smile, she walked toward him, glanced at the warrior knight still awaiting a command and said, "I think it should be something more human."

Interesting. He would have thought she'd play into the magical fantasy. "Like what?"

"Does he have a love interest?" She moved up beside him.

Tanner took a deep breath of that warm, citrusy scent and forced his gaze to the screen. "Of course. The Lady Gwen."

"Oooh, I like that."

"Ten-year-old boys won't, but hopefully everyone else will," he told her wryly.

She laughed and the sound was musical, soft, as enchanting as the magical game he was working on.

"So then," she said, leaning down, bracing her hands on the edge of his desk, "if the knight kills the troll with the enchanted sword, then Lady Gwen is swept into a dimensional prison."

Tanner blinked at her. He hadn't been expecting that. *"What?"*

She laughed again. "It makes sense, doesn't it? He does something he *knows* is wrong—I'm guessing the use of the magical element—and so his punishment is to lose what he loves most."

Intrigued, he said, "Hardly fair to Lady Gwen, though."

"Ah, she knew what she was getting into the minute she met Sir Whatever-His-Name-Is."

"Hawk," Tanner told her, thinking about her suggestion. He had to admit, he never would have gone in that direction. But now he was considering it…

"Of course his name is Hawk," she said, grinning. "Very heroic. So, Gwen disappears into a dimensional prison. Or she's sucked into a portal—"

He caught the glint of excitement in her eye and shared it. Funny. Tanner had been designing games for more than ten years. He'd always considered it the perfect profession for him. An isolated one. A career where he didn't require other people around—where he could shut himself up in his own world and create the images that had always been a part of him.

He'd never had a collaborator. Never even considered having one. Now with a quick conversation, Ivy had sparked new ideas in his mind and he knew in his gut, they were good ones.

Having Ivy in the house the last couple of days had surprised him in more ways than he would have expected. Yes, she'd been a distraction. But he'd allowed that distraction to get out of hand, too. He hadn't kept his distance from her. Instead, he'd sought her out. Talking to her as she cooked, helping her move furniture when she had decided that his living room was too sterile-looking.

But the most surprising part of all of this was just how insightful she was about the game he was currently tweaking. She'd had other suggestions for elevating the skill level while maintaining an accessibility that all game makers strive for. And now, she just might have found a way for him to change the ending into something amazing.

"She's trapped despite her powers," he mused aloud, shifting his gaze to the warrior knight before starting a new sketch on the paper in front of him. He picked up a pen and quickly roughed out an image of the Lady Gwen being dragged into a shining doorway that pulsed with energy.

"That's amazing," Ivy whispered and he realized she'd come closer, her hair now brushing his cheek.

He gritted his teeth and kept his gaze locked on his drawing. Was it his fault that Lady Gwen suddenly bore a remarkable resemblance to Ivy?

"God, you're a terrific artist," she said, reaching past him to stroke the tip of one finger along the line of Lady Gwen's flowing gown.

"It's just a rough draft," he told her, noticing just how tight his voice sounded. His pen sketched in a deeply cut bodice on Lady Gwen's dress, displaying the tops of round, high breasts and he couldn't help wondering what Ivy's breasts would look like and feel like in his hands. His mouth.

Tanner's entire body went still. His mind blanked out and all he could see was the mental image of Ivy, stretched across his bed, naked.

Blowing out a breath, he swallowed hard and fought his way back to the conversation. "This is just to give the programmers direction."

"It's still amazing," she argued, "I can't draw a crooked line and you'd think that would be easy. So, how will Lady Gwen get out of the portal?"

Tanner shrugged. "Her knight has to save her."

"Why can't she save herself?"

He sighed and risked a quick glance up at her. But turning his head to hers brought their mouths within a breath of each other. His gaze dropped to her lips and he felt a quick, sharp stab of desire slam into him. His body was hard, instantly. He felt the rush of heat filling his veins and told himself to get a grip.

The problem was, he wanted to get a grip on *her.*

Shaking his head to get rid of those thoughts, Tanner muttered, "This is a video game, not a lesson in equal opportunity."

"But it could be," she said, arguing her point.

"Oh, don't get me wrong, I suppose every woman wants her white knight, whether she'll admit it or not. But what happens when the brave menfolk aren't around? Shouldn't we be strong enough to save ourselves?"

His eyes locked onto hers as he tried to see past her interest in the game to what lay behind her words. Her eyes were soft, but with a shadow in them that looked a lot like old pain. Concern awakened inside him, pushing past the desire still choking him and he heard himself ask, "Speaking from experience? Has your own white knight let you down lately?"

Her smile faded abruptly and those shadows in her eyes darkened before sliding into the background. "I don't have one. A knight, that is. Not anymore."

Pain flickered on her expression and then disappeared again so quickly Tanner wasn't entirely sure he'd seen it at all. But whether he had or not, she clearly didn't want to discuss it and he knew better than anyone how it felt to want to keep your private life private. So he let it go.

For now.

But he knew that sooner or later, he would want to know what—or who—had hurt her. What he didn't know was *why* he needed to know.

"Okay then," he looked back to the sketch in front of him and asked, "So how do you see Lady Gwen escaping on her own?"

"It has to be impressive…"

"Oh," he said, "naturally."

If she heard the sarcasm in his tone, she ignored it.

"What if Lady Gwen is a sorceress? What if she breaks through the portal by wielding a spell that draws on her knight's love for her?"

Tanner thought about that for a moment, then turned back to his sketch pad, his mind alive with ideas. Quick strokes became a drawing rich in detail in no time at all and before he knew it, he and Ivy were brainstorming solutions that were nothing short of brilliant.

He was so caught up in what they were creating together that when she leaned in close again, he almost avoided getting lost in her scent again.

Almost.

"We're nearly finished with the shearing, Ivy." Dan Collins swung one arm out and indicated the back half of the acreage. "We've got a couple teams back there right now."

Ivy frowned a little and squinted out at the trees. It was hard to concentrate on what Dan was saying because she was so exhausted it felt as though there was a fog hanging over her brain. Hadn't gotten much sleep the night before. Mainly because after she'd left Tanner's house, her mind had been so full of him, she hadn't been able to close her eyes without seeing his image.

She'd had a good time with him, darn it. She hadn't counted on actually *liking* the man. And now she was feeling guilty. He was being…nice. And she was lying to him. Tricking him.

"Ivy?" Dan laid one big hand on her shoulder and asked, "You okay?"

"Yeah," she said, forcing a smile, "I'm fine. Just tired."

"Not surprising since you're running back and forth between the farm and the rich guy's place. You sure working for him is a good idea?" In his fifties, Dan looked at her as one of his own kids. He'd been working at the tree farm since before Ivy was born and he knew the place—and her—very well. "You're burning your candle at both ends and in the middle. Girl, you can't run the farm and the gift shop during the day and work for King at night without wearing yourself out."

"I'm fine," she insisted, tipping her head back to let the sunshine beat against her closed eyes. "Really, Dan. You know why I'm working for him."

"I do, but that doesn't mean I like it."

"Now you sound like Mike."

"Smart man."

She tipped her head to one side, opened her eyes and grinned up at Dan. "You two are peas in a pod. I swear I don't know why Pop's worried about leaving me as long as you're around."

But he didn't smile as she'd hoped. Instead, worry lines dug themselves more deeply into the furrow between his eyes.

"We got a right to be worried. All of us. That King fella could make us some serious trouble." His mouth worked as if his words tasted bitter. "All the complaining that man's done about the farm, it's only a matter of time before he does something bigger. Like a lawsuit or something."

Just what Ivy had been worrying about before she'd actually met Tanner. Now, she wasn't so sure.

"I don't think he will," she said, wondering if that was merely wishful thinking. "But turning down the volume on the music can't hurt."

He scowled and shook his head. "Who doesn't like Christmas music? I want to know."

Ivy laughed and tucked her arm through his as she started leading him off in the direction of the shearing crew. "It'll all work out, Dan. Once we pull off the big wedding, we can take care of the more immediate payment. And with the extra money I'm making now, the two weddings we just booked and the birthday parties we have scheduled, I can pay off the bank loan that much sooner and we can continue the expansion."

"I just don't like seeing you work yourself into the ground is all," he muttered.

"I'm fine. Honestly. Now," she said firmly, shifting the subject back to business, "I know we should have had the last of the trees shaped by the first of July, but with things as busy as they are…"

Dan slid into the new conversation gratefully. "Doesn't matter, really. We've got time. The ones we're working on now won't be up for purchase until next year anyway."

Ivy listened, and inspected the trees they passed along the way. The annual shearing was a big job, but it had to be done and at the right time, too. The idea was to cut off new growth as soon as it was developed—before it had a chance to get tough and woody. Shearing controlled the shape and density of the trees themselves.

Took a lot of work to get that perfect, proportional Christmas tree shape. And some of the guys who worked for Angel tree farm were downright territorial over the shearing process. Some preferred working with the Scotch pines and a couple thought the Douglas fir, that didn't really require shearing, was the better tree anyway.

But, Ivy thought, *that's why Angel trees offered a choice.* Everyone had their own idea of the perfect Christmas tree. To her though, they were *all* perfect.

Dan was still talking and she came up out of her own thoughts to pay attention. "Got a good healthy crop up there and the latest batch of Fraser fir seedlings are coming along. The balsam firs are in even better shape. Should be fine over the winter."

"That's good news," she said, letting her gaze slide across the pines and firs they passed along the way. Most of the bigger trees she saw wore brightly colored tags, with the name of their adopted family painted on in script.

Her Adopt-A-Tree program was really starting to catch on.

Scotch pines bristled against her bare arms as she walked past and Ivy noticed the pristine shaping her crews had managed. The scent of evergreen filled her head and wrapped her in a familiar sense of comfort.

She loved all of her trees, of course, but her favorite by far was the Fraser fir. It was the tree her own family always had in the house and she thought personally that no other Christmas tree reached the same stage of perfection. The color, the scent, the height and width. It was as if God Himself had designed the perfect tree. All the Angel family had to do was grow them.

Her sneakers kicked up dirt in the rows between the trees and she idly noticed that it was time to get the crews out to thin the weeds. From a distance, she heard the sound of kids laughing. That was the main reason she loved what she did so much. They weren't just growing and selling trees here. They were making memories for families. Making Christmas as special to everyone else as it was to her.

"Maude says to tell you she sold the Wedding Ring quilt to that young couple from Fresno."

"Oh, that's great," Ivy said, remembering the couple who had wandered the farm area for hours before coming in and booking their wedding. Satisfaction rolled through her but not just for her own operation's success, but the town's, as well. Every piece of handcrafted beauty the shop sold, helped a craftsman in town. And with every job saved, they made Cabot Valley a little more secure.

As they approached the shearing crew, Dan walked on ahead, but Ivy stopped in her tracks. She turned her head and glanced over at Tanner's house. She could just see the roof and chimney from this perspective, and she wondered what he was doing. If he was lonely in his self made prison.

But mostly, she wondered what he would say
if he could see her here.

Where she really belonged.

Five

Ivy's nervous bride was taking a lot of her energy.

Patsy Harrington had lots of ideas, but most of the major decisions had already been made and changing them now was only going to create chaos. In dealing with the brides, Ivy had learned that being firm but supportive was the only real way to survive.

"We talked about this last time, remember?" Ivy pointed to the creek where a new bridge was being constructed. "You wanted to be able to pose for photos at the bridge, with the trees in the background."

"Yes," Patsy said, hitching her designer handbag higher on her shoulder, "but I was thinking that maybe it would be better to be in the middle of the trees instead. That way, we're surrounded by the greenery and our wedding clothes will really pop in the photos."

Ivy gave a small, inward sigh. She had her crew building the very bridge that Patsy had insisted on. And, she didn't really want an entire wedding party trooping through the tree lines. "But, your dress could get ruined that way, too, with the dirt and fertilizer..." She purposely stopped, letting her words trail off so that Patsy would come to the right decision as she considered things.

"True..." The woman chewed at her bottom lip and looked back at the creek and the graceful arch of the soon to be finished bridge. "And it is very pretty down by the stream."

"It is," Ivy agreed. "Plus, as we discussed, we'll have pine boughs attached to the railings with white ribbon and the flowers you selected. "It's a gorgeous spot for pictures, Patsy. Couldn't ask for better."

"I suppose," she said, nodding. Her expertly cut hair swung out from her chin in a graceful arc as she turned back to Ivy. "Okay then, never mind. Honestly, I don't know how you put up with me, Ivy. I'm driving my own mother insane and my fiancé keeps threatening to kidnap me and elope!"

"Oh, can't have that!" Ivy had one brief, hideous vision of the wedding being canceled and her loan coming due. No, no. "The wedding's going to be beautiful, Patsy. You'll see. You've made all the tough decisions, now all you have to do is trust us to pull it together."

"You're right," the woman said, checking her slender wristwatch. "And I should get going. I've got an appointment in town to talk to the florist."

Carol Sands owned the only flower shop in town and hardly ever got he opportunity to show off her artistic abilities. The Harrington wedding was giving the whole town a chance to shine and they were all eager to prove themselves.

"Carol's very excited about doing the flowers for your wedding," Ivy said. "And we all appreciate the fact that you're using the local suppliers this way."

"Only makes sense," Patsy told her as they started walking across the farm toward the front gate. Laughing, she added, "I know I don't seem like it lately, but I'm actually pretty level-headed."

"All brides get a little weirded out at times," Ivy reassured her.

Patsy let her gaze slide across the rows of trees and what looked like endless miles of bright blue sky. "I just loved this place the moment I came across your Web site. And when Tom and I came to look around, I knew this was where I wanted to hold my wedding."

"I'm glad to hear it. I think it's beautiful here, too."

"Oh, it really is," Patsy agreed. "And, since I live in Sacramento, it would be crazy to try and use city florists and musicians when I can get everything I need right here in Cabot Valley."

"Exactly what we love to hear," Ivy told her. This is what she'd been hoping for by expanding her farm. Her friends and neighbors would be part of the enterprise and the entire town would eventually benefit.

The two women continued to talk over plans as they wandered across the farm.

Maybe, Tanner told himself, Mitchell and Ivy were right. Maybe he had been too closed off since he moved to Cabot Valley. Maybe the mistake he'd made when angry about the Christmas tree farm was in going to the sheriff instead of dealing with the owners directly.

He stared out his office window at the swarms of people wandering the farm's long neat rows of trees. From his vantage point, he could see one corner of the parking lot where dozens of cars were clustered behind a partial screen of bushes. It was definitely a booming business that he'd already learned was important to the locals.

So perhaps what he should do, he thought, was talk to the owners. See if they could find a way to work together in this. Not that he was looking to make friends. He still wasn't interested in that, but there was no reason to have an enemy either.

It was early afternoon and he hadn't even begun work yet. What better time to take a walk and meet the neighbors? Before he could talk himself out of it, he headed downstairs.

A few minutes later he was a part of the scene he'd been complaining about for two months. Here, the Christmas carols were impossible to ignore. With the summer sun slamming down onto him, he lost himself in the crowds and caught snatches of conversations as he went.

Kids whining, fathers grumbling, mothers soothing. He smiled in satisfaction that he wasn't one of their number, until it hit him that *he* was the outsider here. Everyone else had a mission. They were there to enjoy each other and their day among the trees. He was alone. As always. The solitary man in an ocean of families and couples.

And for the first time in his life, Tanner didn't care for it.

His smile faded as his gaze swept the area, taking in the tiny café with outdoor seating— not much more than a snack bar, really. The menu was simple. Hot dogs, hamburgers, chips and drinks. But there were plenty of people in line. Just as the gift shop bustled with customers. He shook his head as women left carrying huge bags filled with who knew what. At least that much in life was a certainty, he told himself. Give a woman the chance to shop and she was off and running. Though the women he was accustomed to preferred to shop where items came in pale blue boxes.

Looking around, Tanner could admit to himself that he was really out of his element here. Not only didn't he normally do crowds, but the very idea of being in the thick of Christmas central was absolutely not him. Yet, here he stood and he had to admit that it wasn't as bad as he'd thought it would be. The rise and fall of the voices around him, blending with the inevitable Christmas music wasn't hard to take.

He'd never been to a Christmas tree farm and seeing all the different types of trees spread out in front of him was...pretty. The scent of the pines filled every breath and even in the heat of summer, he got the draw. The appeal. Kids ran up and down the rows, playing in safety in the man-made forest, their squeals of laughter echoing in the air. Parents wandered, keeping an eye on the kids, while clearly enjoying themselves. Tanner wandered, too, wanting to take his time and make up his own mind about this operation before introducing himself to whoever was in charge.

He didn't know a pine from a fir, but he could see that the place was well cared for. There were few weeds growing in the separating rows and a glance at the old farmhouse told him that upkeep was important to the Angel family. The Victorian had to be at least a hundred years old, but its sky blue paint and white trim was tidy. Flower pots sat on the porch railings and hung from hooks attached to the ceiling. Window panes gleamed in the sunlight and the door stood open as if welcoming visitors. He shook his head in wonder that the owners weren't worried about someone walking into the house and stealing them blind. But apparently, small town life was a far cry from life in L.A.

"Can I help you with anything?"

Tanner turned to the younger man smiling at him. "No thanks. Just looking around."

"And you're welcome to. But if you do need something or if you find a tree you want to adopt, you just give a yell, someone will find you."

"Right, thanks." Adopt a tree? What kind of person was it who came up with something like that, anyway? He kept walking and didn't stop again until a little girl of about six stepped out in front of him.

"Mister, can you lift me up?"

He glanced around, looking for the girl's

parents, but there were no other adults nearby. Wasn't anyone watching the kid? He stared down into a pair of big brown eyes and asked, "Why?"

"So I can reach Lisa."

Even more confusing. "Who's Lisa?"

She laughed. "My tree, silly. Her name is Lisa. I got to name her cause Mommy said I could and Daddy said everything should have a name and she's too pretty to just be 'tree'."

"You named your tree?" Tanner could hardy believe he was even having this conversation. But now, like it not, he was sucked in. The tiny girl was all shining innocence, with her pigtails, cuffed Levi's and bright red sneakers.

"Yes, and now Lisa's tag is all turned around," she said, pointing at a wooden disk inside a plastic sleeve, hanging from one of the top branches of the nearest tree. "I don't want somebody else to buy her because she's my tree. My daddy said."

The girl spoke so fast, her words tumbled into each other, but Tanner had gotten the gist of the problem. "I can fix the tag for you," he offered, reaching for it.

"No!" She stopped him with that single word and when he looked again, she was shaking her head hard enough to send her twin pigtails flying. "I have to do it because she's my tree and it's my job. So can you lift me up?"

Tanner frowned when she held up her arms, clearly expecting him to do just as she had asked. He hadn't been around kids since he *was* one, yet he didn't see a way out of helping the girl without looking like a complete jerk. So sighing, he bent down, lifted the child and held her as carefully as he would have a ticking time bomb while she reached out with both hands to turn the plastic-covered tag around.

"See?" she asked, "that's my tree's name right there on the bottom. My name's Ellie and I didn't have room to put me on there, too. So just Lisa's name is on it, but that's okay, don't you think?"

Sure enough, in uneven letters was the word *Lisa* painted in a sunshine yellow. There was also an uneven candy cane done in red and white and a lopsided star in blue. At the top of the tag, an adult had printed the words, *Callendar family.*

"Very nice," Tanner said, looking at the girl in his arms. "Are you finished?"

"Almost," she assured him, and straightened the tag again, turning it so that the artwork was facing out. Then she patted the pine needles and smoothed her little hand right up to the top. "That's where our angel will go at Christmas time. Mommy says it will be a perfect fit, too. Lisa's gonna look so pretty in our house."

"I'm sure she will," he said, shooting a worried glance at the surrounding area, positive that the girl's parents would show up any second and he'd be accused of trying to kidnap the girl or something.

"Do you have your tree picked out yet?"

"What? No," he told her, staring into those brown eyes again. "I don't get a Christmas tree."

Her brow furrowed. "Why not?"

Why? Because Christmas had never been anything but a misery to Tanner. He didn't have lovely childhood memories like this little girl was busily making. He didn't have fond recollections of a happy family gathering. When he thought of Christmas, he thought of empty hotel rooms, a room service menu and a holiday movie on the television. Not exactly something he longed to repeat. But this child didn't need to know any of that—nor would she understand it. Their childhoods were not just years apart—but worlds apart as well.

"I just...don't."

She patted his cheek. "That's why you look sad. I could help you find a good one if you want and then you could be happy again. I always find our trees and Daddy says that I'm best at it."

He didn't know whether to be touched or appalled that a little girl was feeling sorry for him.

"Thanks, but—"

"Ellie?"

Thank God, Tanner thought, turning at the sound of the woman's voice. He was still holding the little girl, still standing stiffly, as if half afraid to move.

"Hi, Mommy! This man helped me fix Lisa's tag so no one else can buy her!"

A pretty woman with light brown hair and eyes just like her daughter's stepped up beside them. She gave him a measuring stare and then must have decided he wasn't a danger because she relaxed and smiled. "That was nice of him, sweetie. But we've got to go now. Daddy's waiting for us with hot dogs and cookies."

"Oh, boy! You can put me down now, mister."

Almost surprised to find he was still holding the girl, Tanner reacted immediately and set her on her feet.

"Thanks a lot," Ellie told him as she slipped her hand into her mother's.

"Yes, thank you," her mom said. "I hope she wasn't a bother."

"No," he told her, realizing it was only the truth. "Not at all."

Both mother and daughter gave him brilliant smiles, then they walked off, hand in hand, toward the snack bar and the lucky man waiting for them.

Lucky man, Tanner mused. Funny, not so long ago, he would have thought a married man with kids was more to be pitied than envied. But now, he thought having a child like the precocious Ellie might not be a terrible thing.

Stunned at the stray thought, he told himself it was probably Ivy's influence. The woman was relentlessly cheerful and optimistic. Clearly some of that was wearing off on him. And he wasn't entirely sure how he felt about that.

Continuing on through the forest of trees, he nodded at people he passed and even began humming along to one of those insidious carols. When he realized what he was doing he stopped, but the fact that he'd hummed along to it at all surprised him. *Was it some sort of brainwashing?* he wondered. Play Christmas music all day every day until it gets to even the most hardened of hearts?

Well, he'd never thought of himself as having a hard heart. Still, in comparison to those who thought Angel Christmas Tree Farm was a paradise, he probably sensed the Scrooge Mitchell had named him. Uncomfortable with that particular label, he shrugged it off. He wasn't *that* bad, he assured himself.

As he stepped out into a patch of sunlight Tanner saw that the full grown trees were now behind him. Ahead of him, were shorter versions and beyond them, were rows and rows of seedlings, barely a foot high. The farm was laid out well, he thought, recognizing the planning and the care that had gone into the Angel Christmas Tree Farm.

While he swept the area with a cool gaze, he stopped when he spotted a familiar blond head walking with a pretty brunette. Ivy and the other woman couldn't have looked more different from each other. Ivy wore jeans, a T-shirt and boots while the brunette wore a short-sleeved silk blouse with gray slacks and a pair of heels that were completely inappropriate for walking through trees.

What was Ivy doing here?

As they came nearer, she looked up and spotted him. His heart did a hard roll and crash in his chest that disturbed him a little. And if he was any judge, she didn't look real happy to see him, a fact that irritated him more than a little. Still, too late now to back out, so he walked to join them.

"Tanner," Ivy said, pleasure in her voice, "I didn't expect to see you over here."

"I could say the same thing to you," he admitted, then shifted his gaze to the brunette. "Am I interrupting something?"

"No," Ivy told him, then said, "Patsy Harrington, this is our neighbor, Tanner King. Tanner, Patsy is here to talk about her upcoming wedding."

"Lovely to meet you," Patsy said, then quickly added, "but I'm afraid I have to run. The florist awaits. Ivy, thanks again for talking me off the ledge."

"No problem," Ivy told her, and Tanner was struck by the warm smile on her face. "Happy to help. Any time."

"You may regret that," Patsy told her with a laugh, then gave Tanner a sly look before grinning at Ivy. "You don't have to walk me out. You two go ahead."

"What was that about?" he asked.

"Oh, nothing." Ivy smiled at him. "She's just nervous about her wedding and wanting to change everything around at the last minute."

"Well, that's irrational," he said.

"No, that's a bride," Ivy told him. "But I talked her out of it. Really, all she wants is reassurance that everything's going to come off beautifully."

"And is it?" he asked, looking into her eyes.

"It will even if I have to do it all by myself," she said firmly. She paused as if considering something, then admitted, "Angel Christmas Tree Farm took a big loan out for the expansion.

There's a big payment due soon. The Harrington wedding is going to take care of that. If anything goes wrong…"

He frowned, both at the proprietary way she was talking about the farm and at the worry in her voice. "What?"

She looked around at the all the trees and sighed. "We could lose the farm."

Interesting, Tanner thought. So the farm was in danger of going under if it couldn't pay back a loan. Then what she'd said hit him and he asked, *"We?"*

Ivy looked at him. "I mean, we as in, we who work here."

"So…what? Housekeeper, Christmas tree farm worker and bridal consultant?"

She shrugged. "Keeps me busy."

"Yeah." He wasn't sure what it was, but something was definitely off here.

"You know, small town. Take work where you can get it."

She looked more uncomfortable than he'd ever seen her and Tanner couldn't help but wonder why. Was she embarrassed that he'd discovered she worked more than one job? She shouldn't be. He had nothing but respect for hardworking people. "What do you do here?"

"Oh, a little bit of everything, I guess," she said, a little vaguely. "Whatever needs doing. Shearing the trees, watering, weed removal when they get bad." She kicked the toe of her boot at one of the offending weeds. "You know, farm stuff."

"Right. And wedding planning." He studied her and noticed that her gaze hadn't met his squarely since the first moment she'd spotted him. Strange behavior for the most upfront, unafraid of confrontation woman he'd ever known.

"But what are you doing over here?" she countered. "I thought you pretty much considered this place enemy territory."

Yeah, he had. Now though, standing in this forest of neatly tended trees with the sound of children's laughter ringing out around him, he couldn't really remember why.

"Well, I started thinking and realized that you might have been right about something."

"I like it already," she said.

"I'm sure," he said wryly. He'd never known a woman yet who didn't love hearing that she was right about something. "Anyway, you said I should have talked to the farm owner and I realized that you had a point. Thought that before I try to find the owner though, I should look around. Get a feel for the place."

"And, what do you think of it?"

He nodded, letting his gaze slide across the area as he said, "It's...nice. I met a little girl, helped her fix the name tag on her tree."

Ivy smiled at him. "That's part of the Adopt-a-Tree program." She started walking back toward the front of the farm and Tanner fell into step beside her, listening as she continued.

"The wooden ornaments are just used for identifying tags now. That's why they're in plastic sleeves, to protect them from the weather. But when the families come to cut down the tree, the tags go home with them as a keepsake ornament."

"Ellie did seem proud of the job she did on it," he mused.

Ivy laughed. "All of the kids are. And you wouldn't believe the different artwork they come up with. I've seen everything from daisies to space aliens on those tags."

"Well sure," Tanner said, "Merry Christmas Aliens."

"You got it," she agreed, laughing. "Anyway, we've got a craft table set up in the gift shop. The kids decorate the tags, then go out with their families to choose their tree. They get to hang the first symbolic ornament on it to stake their claim."

He'd picked up on one word in that description. "*We* have a craft table?"

She shrugged. "Well, I just meant *we* as in Angel Christmas Tree Farm. Anyway, most families tend to make a day of it when they're here to choose their trees. They come and have lunch, let the kids paint and then head into the farm to look for the perfect Christmas tree."

He lifted his gaze to the trees they passed. "They all look pretty perfect to me."

"Isn't that a nice thing to say. And here I thought you hated Christmas."

"Hard to hate a tree," he said.

"There might be hope for you yet," Ivy said, turning her face up to his. He stared into her blue eyes and felt something in his chest tighten. When a slow smile curved her mouth, that tightness became almost unbearable.

All he could think about was grabbing her and kissing her until the deep, raw hunger inside him was eased. But he couldn't do that here and now. So the only safe bet was to keep moving.

"Since you work here," he asked, "can you take a break and show me around?"

"I'd love to."

"You won't get in trouble with the boss?"

Her mouth quirked. "I think the boss will understand." She tucked her arm through his and he felt the heat of her body pressed against him. "What do you want to see first?"

Her naked, but that probably wasn't what she meant. So he dialed back on the desire pumping through him and decided to assuage a different kind of hunger for the moment.

"Honestly," he admitted, "how about the snack bar? Ever since I got here, I've been smelling those hot dogs."

"No wonder you're hungry. You're awake early today. I'm not even due at your place for another three hours."

"Yeah," he said, his gaze caught on the way the sunlight played on her hair. "I seem to be doing that more and more lately."

Her smile widened. "I'm glad. You should see the sun occasionally, Tanner. Don't want to turn into a mole."

He didn't say anything, but privately, he knew the reason for his switch in hours had nothing to do with sunlight. It was all about seeing her. Spending more time with her when she was at the house. Listening to her and laughing with her.

And as he followed after her on the way to the snack stand, his gaze dropped to the curve of her behind and he told himself that getting up earlier certainly had its perks.

Six

Ivy was finally starting to relax enough to enjoy having Tanner on her farm. When she had first spotted him standing in the sunshine, Ivy's heart had nearly stopped. In a flash, dozens of thoughts had rushed through her mind, most of them revolving around how to keep him from finding out *she* owned the farm. But she needn't have worried after all. Her employees all knew that she was working part time for Tanner. And they knew why.

She glanced up at him as they walked slowly down a row of Scotch pines. His gaze was sharp and constantly moving. He was taking it all in and she couldn't help wondering what he thought of her home. Of her family's pride and joy.

But she couldn't ask. Couldn't even hint at her real identity—which went against the grain for her. She hated lying. And for the first time since she'd met him, Ivy had actually *lied* to Tanner. Before, it had all been omissions, just keeping quiet about the truth. Now, she'd been forced to actively lie and she wasn't very comfortable with that.

Still, she couldn't see that she had any choice, so she was trying to make the best of the situation. Now that she had him on her turf, she was going to take full advantage of it. They shared hot dogs and sodas, then she took him on a tour of the gift shop. One of the girls working the shop had taken one look at Tanner and practically melted on the spot. But then, Ivy couldn't blame Kathy for that, she supposed, since she felt the same way. Every time she got anywhere close to Tanner, her body lit up like a summer fireworks show.

As that thought settled in her mind, Ivy felt the slightest twinge of guilt ping inside her before she shut it down. She wasn't exactly in charge of her own body's chemical reaction to the man, after all. It wasn't as if she could turn it on and off at will. Still, she told herself to ignore the buzz of sensation his nearness caused. She wasn't looking for love—or even a fling, for that matter. What she needed from Tanner was far more important. She needed him to stop threatening everything she loved.

They wandered the gift store and she pointed out the kids' craft table where little Ellie had made her ornament tag. There were a couple of geniuses busily at work, but they ignored all the adults in the room. He seemed amazed by the crafts made by the women in town, and asked enough questions that Ivy knew he was paying attention. There were hand-poured candles and scented soaps wrapped in ribbon and stacked in baskets. There were rugs and placemats and afghans, blown glass vases and wine glasses.

"And the women in town made all of this?" he asked.

"Mostly," she said. "But Dave Benoit made the glassware. He's got a glass house behind his place. He designs and makes everything himself."

"Impressive," he said, turning to look around the shop, his gaze moving over both merchandise and customers. "And the store's open all year, too?"

"We are now."

One of his eyebrows lifted.

Immediately, she winced and corrected herself. "I mean, the Angel family figured if the shop was open all year, it would give their customers more reason to come and help out the local craftspeople at the same time."

He looked at her, his dark blue eyes locking with hers and Ivy felt that stir of something deliciously primal rise up inside her again. The guilt she was half expecting didn't show and she was grateful. She hadn't set out to entice Tanner and certainly hadn't been looking for a lover, but there was something about this one man that made her feel…

"So!" She swallowed hard and forced a smile she knew wasn't a convincing one. Oh, she didn't want to think about what Tanner made her feel. That was a one-way trip to crazytown and she just didn't have the time for it.

Or the heart. She wasn't the kind of girl for one night stands and easy, see-you-later sex. She was the girl next door. Literally.

"Am I making you nervous?" he asked.

Ivy laughed shortly and shook her head. "What a silly question, of course you don't."

"Uh-huh. Then why are you backing away from me?"

Damn it. She was. She'd instinctively taken two or three steps away from him and wouldn't you know that he'd notice.

"I was just…" She huffed out a breath. "Never mind. Come on, I'll show you the rest."

His lips curved a little and Ivy glowered. As he walked past her toward the door, she shot a look at Kathy and her mother, Anne, working the counter. Anne gave her two thumbs up and a wink which only made Ivy feel worse. Now not only was she lying to Tanner, but her friends were co-conspirators. Oh, this was getting tangled up fast.

And it wasn't helping that her body felt both loose and tightly wound all at once.

Determined to get past her own body's reaction to the man, Ivy kept a smile plastered to her face as she continued their tour. Proudly, she showed him the brides' dressing room, outfitted with three way mirrors and a lovely bathroom where a woman could get dressed for her wedding in comfort. Then she took him to the meadow and the fast moving creek to show him their most popular wedding scenes.

Finally, she stopped at the area set aside for kids' birthday parties. There, the inflated, castle-shaped bounce house stood, waiting only for children to step inside and play. The freshly painted white picket fence around the huge red and yellow bouncing palace was closed though, keeping unsupervised kids out.

They were far enough away from the main area of the farm that they were pretty much alone. Christmas music continued sighing from the overhead speakers, but the sounds of voices were muted and at a distance. Now that they were away from other distractions, Ivy felt a little nervous and her body once again started clamoring for his touch. She took a breath and reached out to grab hold of the fence as if holding onto it would keep her from reaching for him.

God, what was going on with her?

Tanner moved in close to her. Laying one hand on the fence top, he said, "I'm surprised kids want to escape from here to climb my trees."

"You know little boys. They always want to do what they're not supposed to."

"I guess." He looked around. "Why don't they have this open for the kids all the time?"

"It wouldn't be special then, would it?" Ivy asked and flipped the latch on the gate. She swung it wide and stepped onto the neatly tended lawn surrounding the bounce house.

Tanner followed in after her and she closed the gate firmly after them.

"They open it up for kids on Saturdays, and then of course, it's the star attraction of the birthday parties."

He tipped his head back to look up at the red, yellow and orange inflated structure, noting the flags attached to the topmost towers fluttering in the warm breeze. "I suppose this thing's a huge hit with the party crowd."

"Oh yeah." She walked toward the castle and gave it a pat. "Have you ever been in one?"

He laughed shortly and gave her a look that said she was clearly out of her mind. "No."

"You want to?"

"What?"

Ivy laughed at the astonishment on his face. Here, she'd been making herself insane over the physical attraction she felt for him. But now, she realized it went deeper than that. She was drawn to more than his sexy appeal. There was something in his eyes that pulled at her, too. It was that careful vulnerability, she thought, looking up at him. There was something about him that told her he'd spent his life being serious. Controlled. And there was a huge part of her that wanted to break through the walls he'd erected so carefully around himself.

Maybe she really was crazy, but if ever a man needed to learn how to have fun, it was Tanner King. He was too alone. Too somber. Too cut off from everything that made life worth living.

And in the last few days, she'd begun to care about him, she realized. More than the sexual heat she felt around him, she actually enjoyed spending time with him and she hated thinking of him all alone in that big, beautiful house. She hated knowing that when she left him, there was nothing to keep him company but the echo of his own voice.

She'd started this whole thing for her own sake. To save her family's legacy and to help her hometown grow and prosper. Now, it was more than that. Sure, she still wanted to protect Angel Christmas Tree Farm and Cabot Valley. But she also wanted to—what? *Save* Tanner King? That thought rattled her a little.

Was she picking up the mantle of Lady Gwen trying to help her knight?

"You can't be serious," he said, looking from her to the bounce house and back again.

"Why not?" she asked, liking the idea more by the minute. Anything that would shake this so stolid man up was a good thing, right? And the fact that it would be just the two of them inside that inflated fun house had nothing to do with it.

She looked around, saw that there was no one nearby and then shifted her gaze back to Tanner. "Come on. Give it a try."

"It's for kids."

"It's for *fun*," she corrected. "I've been in it lots of times."

Alternately hopping on first one foot then the other, she tugged off her boots, then tossed them to the grass. Fisting her hands at her hips, she tossed her hair out of her eyes and challenged, "Well?"

He shook his head and muttered, "You're crazy."

"That's been said before."

She turned her back on him and crawled into the bounce house. She was betting that he wouldn't be able to resist the challenge of joining her. Once inside, she looked at him through the orange mesh wall and laughed aloud. "Come on, Tanner. Live a little. Or are you scared?"

He snorted. "Are you seriously *daring* me? What are you, twelve?"

Oh, she didn't feel like a twelve-year-old, Ivy admitted silently as she watched him. Those long legs of his looked amazing in his jeans and the breadth of his shoulders made her want to strip off his dark blue T-shirt and run her hands over what she guessed was a hard, sculpted chest.

Her mouth went dry.

Nope.

No twelve-year-olds here.

"Are you turning down the dare?" she countered. "What are you…chicken?"

His eyes went wide and he laughed shortly. "You're like nobody I've ever met before."

She swayed in place unsteadily and wasn't sure if it was the inflated floor making her knees wobble—or if it was the gleam in his eyes. "Thank you."

"Not sure it was a compliment."

"I am." She walked backward, her socks sliding a little on the puffy rubber. It wasn't easy keeping her balance in the bounce house at the best of times. Now, with Tanner's influence, it was turning into quite the chore.

She watched him, holding her breath as she waited to see what he would decide. And then she blew out an expectant breath as he shook his head and toed off his black tennis shoes.

"This is crazy," he muttered, bending low to climb into the structure.

"And you don't do crazy?" she taunted, bouncing a little to unsteady him.

"Not generally," he agreed, standing up and bracing his legs wide apart. He glanced around then looked at her. "Okay, now what?"

"Now we bounce." Ivy jumped as high as she could, then landed and watched the resulting wave knock Tanner off balance.

He caught himself, staggered a little and narrowed his eyes on her. "Want to play rough, do you?"

"Whatever it takes," she said and jumped again.

"Challenge accepted." He took a flying leap, landed on his backside and the bounce knocked Ivy right off her feet.

In a hot second, Tanner was beside her. She looked up into his dark blue eyes and shivered at the hard glitter shining in those depths. He braced his hands on either side of her head and his knees on either side of her hips.

God, he was so close. His mouth just a breath from hers. His big, warm body so tantalizingly near.

Then he smiled and sent a flurry of butterfly wings erupting in the pit of her stomach.

"Lose your balance, Ivy?"

She was really afraid she had. Only it wasn't

the kind of balance he was talking about. No, this balance was the delicate art of stabilizing her emotions that she'd been practicing for four years. Ever since David had died. She'd been going through the motions, living her life, doing her chores, laughing, talking and never once actually *living*. Now, thanks to Tanner King, her body and heart were waking up and it was nearly painful.

So she ignored that rush of feelings, determined to blank them out and keep them at bay. She'd think about all of that later, when there was time to examine what she was feeling and decide how she felt about it. For now, she gave herself up to the moment.

"Not for long," she answered and shoved him hard enough that he fell backward and rolled to one side.

She scrambled to her feet and ran across the wobbling floor to the opposite corner. Her hair slipped free of its ponytail and hung about her shoulders. She whipped it back and out of her way as she watched Tanner stealthily approach, that same desire-filled glint shining in his eyes.

Jumping up and down in place, she made sure his pace was inelegant and difficult. He fought to keep his balance and still kept coming, his gaze never leaving hers. *This might not have been such a good idea,* she told herself as her stomach did somersaults and her blood pressure skyrocketed. Her heartbeat raced and every square inch of her body blossomed with heat as if in anticipation.

"You know," he said, his voice a low rumble of sound that seemed to scramble her nerve endings, "I'm beginning to like this place."

"Good," she said, forcing cheerful innocence into her voice. "I'm glad you're having fun."

"Oh, I intend to have even more fun in a second or two," he promised and his eyes swept her up and down before finally locking onto hers.

"Um, Tanner, maybe we should…"

He jumped, landed about a foot in front of her and the resulting wave pelted her off her feet and tossed her at him. Instantly, Tanner's arms came around her.

Ivy's breath left her in a rush and she had to struggle to draw in more air. Her body was pinned along his and his strong arms held her in place so that even if she'd wanted to escape—which she really didn't—she would have had a hard time of it.

Her breasts were crushed against his chest and her nipples went hard and sensitive. Instinctively, she rubbed against him and when she heard him hiss in a breath, she knew he was feeling exactly what she was. Her core went hot and damp, and everything in her…yearned.

He lifted one hand, brushed her hair back from her face and then smoothed his palm down the line of her jaw, her throat. Everywhere he touched her, licks of flame erupted. Ivy had never experienced anything like it. She'd never known this kind of frenzied need that was clawing at her, demanding more.

"You make me want to throw the rules away,"

he murmured and dipped his head to brush his lips to her forehead.

She sucked in a breath. "Rules?"

"Doesn't matter," he said, shaking his head. "You've been making me a little nuts the last few days."

"I have?"

He smiled and the curve of his mouth sent tiny electrical shocks blasting through her system.

"Yeah. And you know it," he said softly. "Every woman knows when she's driving a man crazy with want."

"Want?"

Oh God yes, she thought. Want was good. Want was very good.

"I like your hair down," he told her, running his fingers through the heavy mass, scraping his short nails across her scalp.

Ivy sighed and closed her eyes.

"I like how you feel in my arms," he admitted.

"I like it, too."

"Good," he said, voice a low throb of need,

"because I want more of it. I want more of *you.*"

Her eyes flew open in time to see him lower his head and slant his lips over hers.

The kiss staggered Ivy. All of her preconceptions, all of her idle daydreaming splintered under the reality of his mouth on hers. His lips were soft yet firm and unyielding. He parted her lips with his tongue and claimed her more intimately, more deeply.

While he explored her mouth, his hands went on a searching mission of their own. He ran his palms up and down her spine and then to the curve of her rear where he held on tightly and pulled her closer against him. She moaned when she felt the hardness of his body pressing into hers and she squirmed as if trying to get even closer. She clung to his shoulders as if holding on for dear life and when her feet shifted on the inflated floor, she felt him move with her.

Her tongue tangled with his in a dance of desperate hunger that shattered her resolve, disintegrated her good intentions. Here was the heat that had drawn her to him from the beginning. Here was the need that had kept her awake nights, wondering what it would be like to touch him and be touched.

Tanner groaned and dropped them both to the floor. He held her cradled against him and when they landed on the cool rubber floor, they rolled, still locked together. Over and under him, she felt her body springing into life as it hadn't for more than four years.

His kiss demanded everything she had to give and she offered it to him gladly. His hands moved as he brought them to a stop, pinned against the inflatable wall. He slid one hand beneath the hem of her T-shirt and she gasped at the exquisite feel of his skin on hers.

His fingertips traced their way up her body until he reached the edge of her bra, then he pushed it up and out of the way and covered her breast with his palm.

"Tanner…" She arched into him, sighing his name.

"Oh yeah," he whispered, his thumb and

forefinger twisting and teasing her sensitive nipple. "This is what I've wanted since the day I saw you, Ivy."

"Me, too. Oh, me, too," she admitted, opening her eyes to look up into his. "Taste me, Tanner. I want to feel your mouth on me."

His eyes flared with raw hunger. He didn't say a word, only dipped his head to her breast and took her nipple into his mouth. Lips and teeth and tongue tortured her gently with sensations that coursed through her with rocketlike speed.

She twisted beneath him, unable to hold still. She lifted one hand to the back of his head and held him there, as if afraid he might stop. And oh, she didn't want him to stop.

The world fell away. All that mattered was this moment. Tanner's mouth on her body. His hot breath brushing her skin.

She wanted more and she wanted it now. Ivy forgot all about where they were. Forgot about the tree farm. Forgot that Tanner King was the one man who had the power to shut down her family's business. Forgot everything, in fact, in favor of concentrating solely on what his touch could do to her.

As if he heard her thoughts, he skimmed his hand down her belly and beneath the waistband of her jeans.

Sunlight beat against Ivy's closed eyelids and she took a breath and held it as Tanner's fingers moved beneath the elastic band of her panties and continued down, to the heart of her torment.

He touched her once and she shattered, body trembling, breath exploding from her lungs. But it wasn't enough for him, he wanted to take her higher.

"Again, Ivy," he whispered, lifting his head from her breast to look down at her. "Break for me again."

She slid her hands up his muscular arms to his shoulders and then dug her fingertips in and held on as her legs parted for him, making room, welcoming his touch.

He dipped one finger inside her and she

shivered. Then he withdrew that finger and entered her again in a slow, gliding rhythm that tore at already sensitized nerves. Her hips rocked into him as he gave and demanded all at once. She felt tension building within and embraced it.

Her gaze locked with his as she felt another climax approaching. She stared into his eyes as the first ripples of pleasure rocked her.

"Tanner!" Her voice was strained and quiet.

"Let go, Ivy," he ordered. "Let go and feel me."

She did.

She had no choice.

Maybe, she thought wildly as she trembled and shook in the safety of his arms, she hadn't had a choice from the first moment she'd walked into his house. Maybe every step they'd taken together had brought them here, to this moment.

Then he kissed her, swallowing her wrenching moans and she stopped thinking entirely.

When the last of her climax faded away, she felt both weak and energized. Her body was alive in a way she'd never experienced before and though she acknowledged another twinge of guilt at the thought, she couldn't deny it.

Tanner pulled his hand free, then tugged her T-shirt down over her breasts. Still looking into her eyes, he said, "This is just the beginning. You know that, right?"

She swallowed hard and fought down a rising tide of desire. Already, her body wanted more.

"Yes, I know," she agreed softly.

"Good." He sat up and drew her with him.

Late afternoon sunshine played through the mesh walls and lay tiny checkerboard patterns over his face. A soft wind sighed through the trees and lifted her hair from her neck. But the breeze didn't do a thing toward damping the fires he'd stirred inside her. She was burning up, aching for his touch and she could see in his eyes that he was feeling the same way.

"Tonight, Ivy," he said, lifting one of her hands to his mouth. He trailed the tip of his tongue across her knuckles and smiled when she shivered in response. "Tonight, I want it all. I want you in my bed, naked."

Her stomach spun and her throat closed up tight. It was a wonder she could breathe, let alone speak. But somehow, she managed. "Tonight, Tanner. I want you inside me."

His eyes flared. "Glad to know we're on the same page."

"Oh yeah." She leaned toward him to give him a kiss to seal their deal, when a too-familiar, outraged voice stopped her cold.

"Ivy! What the hell are you doing?"

Seven

"Mike!" Ivy sounded both shocked and horrified.

Tanner sent a quick look toward the speaker and spotted an older man, gray hair bristling, pale blue eyes narrowed, standing on the outside of the bounce house, glaring in at them.

"What the hell's going on, Ivy?" the older man demanded again.

She hurried to her feet, tossed one anxious glance at Tanner and then scuttled wobbly across the floor. "I didn't know you were here," she said.

"Yeah, well I could say the same." The old guy looked past Ivy to glare at Tanner. "I heard a ruckus. Thought I should check it out. So you want to tell me what's happening?"

"Not really," she said, half turning as Tanner walked up behind her. "Um, Mike Angel, this is Tanner King. Tanner, this is Mike."

Well hell.

The owner of the tree farm, Tanner thought. No wonder Ivy was acting so weird. She'd just been caught by her boss and she was probably embarrassed. Plus, he thought, the old man looked mad enough to fire her and Tanner couldn't let that happen.

See, his brain taunted, *this* is what happens when you relax your rules. When you forget to keep your distance from people. But even though he knew his brain was absolutely right, he couldn't really regret what had just happened between them. In fact, he was looking forward very much to more rule-breaking as soon as he could get her to his house.

For the moment however, they had to get out of this situation.

"Good to meet you, sir," he said and would have extended his hand, but for the mesh wall separating them.

"I'll bet," Mike Angel told him, then shifted his gaze back to Ivy. "You come on out of there now."

"Right." She gave Tanner a quick look that said she wasn't going to argue with the man and hoped he wouldn't either.

Tanner wasn't going to argue, he assured himself. But he also wasn't going to be treated like a ten-year-old caught throwing a baseball through a window, either.

Ivy dropped to her hands and knees and slipped out the doorway of the bounce house to sit on the grass so she could tug her boots back on. Tanner was right behind her.

"So you gonna tell me why you're rolling around in the kid's play palace?"

Ivy flushed and Tanner was struck by it. He couldn't remember the last time he'd seen a

woman blush with embarrassment. Hell, he
hadn't been sure they were capable of it anymore. But Ivy, he'd already discovered, was like
no other woman he'd ever known.

"I was giving Tanner a tour of the farm
and—"

"Just what kind of tour was this?" Mike
asked.

Tanner wasn't the kind of man to stand by
and have a woman defend him—even when
he needed defending, which he didn't. They
hadn't done anything wrong. Although, Ivy's
boss might not be too happy with her. And that
worried Tanner a bit. He wouldn't want to see
her lose her job over this.

He felt more himself once he had his shoes
on and was standing on ground that didn't
ripple and shift beneath him. The fact that he
towered over the older man didn't hurt either.
Still, this was Ivy's employer and the owner of
the farm he'd been complaining about for two
months. Maybe, he thought, that was part of
why the older man looked less than welcoming.

After several visits from the sheriff, who could blame him?

"Tanner King," he said, holding out one hand to the man.

Mike Angel looked at his extended hand but instead of taking it, turned his gaze on Ivy. "Anything you want to tell me, Ivy girl?"

"Not a thing, Mike," she said honestly. Pushing her hair back behind her ears. "I just thought you'd want me to see that Tanner here got a good look at the farm."

"Uh-huh."

Tanner let his hand drop and accepted that the older man wasn't happy about his being there. Still, he wasn't used to being ignored and found he didn't care for it much. "I asked Ivy to show me around, Mr. Angel. She gave me a tour of the farm and when we ended up here, I suggested we try out the bounce house."

Ivy shot him a grateful, if surprised look, as he took responsibility for slipping into the inflated palace.

He ignored it and focused instead on the older

man watching him through shrewd eyes. "She's shown me your whole operation here and I've got to say it's impressive."

"Is that right?" Mike's gaze measured him and Tanner felt like a kid standing in front of the principal's desk.

"It is," he said, refusing to be cowed by the steely look in his adversary's eyes. But at the same time, he wanted to smooth things over so that Ivy wouldn't be in any kind of trouble. "Look," he said, "I realize you and I got off to a bad start."

"Didn't get off to any kind of start at all, Mr. King," Mike countered. "Since you decided to go to the police with your complaints instead of coming directly to me. Seems to me a man might come and talk to another man face-to-face if he has a problem. Rather than going to the sheriff over and over again."

Mitchell had been right about that, Tanner told himself with an inner grumble. He hadn't done himself any good at all by complaining to the local police instead of simply talking to his neighbor. But in his own defense, Tanner *never* met his neighbors. Hell, he'd lived in his condo in L.A. for five years and wouldn't have been able to recognize his neighbors in a lineup.

"Mike…" Ivy sounded worried and the tone in her voice had Tanner nodding.

"No, Ivy, he's right." He met the older man's eyes and thought he spotted a flash of admiration there. Why that made him feel better, he couldn't have said. "Mr. Angel, I should have come to you from the start. That was my mistake. Maybe we could have worked things out between us without getting the police involved."

"Well now," the older man mused thoughtfully, "call me Mike. I got respect for a man who can admit he's done wrong." He held out his right hand and waited to see if Tanner would take it.

He did. The old man had a hard, firm grip that spoke of years of physical labor as he squeezed Tanner's hand briefly. And the look in his eyes clearly said he was short of patience and damn curious about just what had been going on before he showed up.

Thinking about that rekindled fires inside Tanner that would be better off left to smolder at the moment. There'd be time enough later to pick up where he and Ivy had left off.

"Anyway," Tanner said abruptly, shattering the strained silence, "I wanted to thank you for letting Ivy show me around. I wouldn't want her to get into trouble for taking time from her work."

"Is that right?" Mike murmured, shifting his gaze to Ivy.

She squirmed a little, obviously uncomfortable with the conversation. She and Mike stared at each other for a long minute before the older man looked back to Tanner.

"It's no trouble," he said. "Glad she took you around. But now, it's time we both got back to work."

"Of course." Tanner nodded and said, "I should get back myself. Ivy, thanks for the tour. Mike, good to meet you."

"You, too. Now, you have any other problems with the farm, you let us know."

"I will," he assured him. "And I appreciate your turning the music down."

"That was Ivy's idea," he said.

Tanner's gaze shifted to her. She'd gone out of her way to try to make things better for him and hadn't said anything about it. Ivy was, he told himself, an intriguing woman. As he stared into her eyes, he let her know, without a word spoken, that he was leaving now, but would be waiting for her later. He wanted her now more than he had before and if he had to wait much longer, it was going to drive him over the edge.

Her eyes flashed in acceptance of his silent message and he knew they were at least on the same page about some things.

"Then I guess I owe you my thanks for making things quieter around here," he finally told her.

"Guess you do," she said, her eyes gleaming with the knowledge of what they'd shared and what was to come.

"I'll have to find a way to show you my appreciation, then won't I?"

"I look forward to it," she said softly.

Tanner left it at that. Giving Mike a brisk nod, he walked off toward the front of the farm and the road that would take him to his place.

He hadn't gone far when Mike grabbed his granddaughter's arm and tugged her further off. "What in the hell are you up to, Ivy?"

"Oh, Pop," she said with a sigh, "this is getting more confusing every day."

"You're playing with fire, Ivy."

"What?" She whipped her head up to look at him. "What do you mean?"

He laughed. "You know damn well what I mean. You're getting in over your head with that man and you know it."

Her grandfather always had been able to see into her heart and mind. It had always made keeping secrets from him nearly impossible and apparently, nothing had changed.

"I didn't start out to," she said.

"Yeah, well you remember what the road to hell is paved with…"

"…good intentions, yes, I know," she said, walking beside her grandfather as he headed off toward the seedling rows. "I was going to tell him who I am, Pop. Really. At least, I've been thinking about telling him. But now, it's complicated."

"Always is when you start lying. By the time you get around to the truth, the lies are so big you can't see a way around them."

"You're not exactly being comforting, you know."

He laughed again and threw one arm over her shoulders. "I'm not trying to be. You don't need comfort, Ivy. You need to straighten this mess out, that's all."

"That's all." She sighed again and let her gaze slide across the familiar scenes around her. "When he finds out the truth, he'll be furious. And he's warming up to the tree farm, but he's not exactly a fan yet, so there's still the chance that he'll sic his lawyer on us and we'll still be up the proverbial creek."

"Seems to not be as angry as he once was," Mike said softly as he slid her a sidelong look. "You wouldn't know the reason for that, would you?"

Ivy groaned. "Just how much did you see?"

"Not much, thank you God for not striking me blind." Mike held up one hand when she opened her mouth to talk. "It's none of my business anyway, honey. You're all grown up. You can make your own decisions. I just want to know that you know what you're doing. That you've got your eyes open wide."

"I'd like to know that, too," she admitted.

The trouble was, she told herself as she tipped her head back and stared up at the white clouds scuttling across a bright blue sky, she just wasn't sure. When she'd started all of this, it had been with the idea of getting to know Tanner, easing him into small town life and hoping that once she'd accomplished the task, he'd stop giving the tree farm so much grief.

But it had stopped being solely about that days ago. She hadn't admitted it to herself, but that was the honest truth. Sunlight speared out from behind a cloud and looked like golden fingers reaching down from the sky. She sighed and the wind carried the sound away.

"I don't have to leave tomorrow," Mike said softly, as if sensing the turmoil within her. "I can stay awhile yet."

She smiled and lowered her gaze to meet his. God, that was tempting. Keep her grandfather here as moral support while she stumbled head first into an affair that probably shouldn't happen. Because she knew that even if Pop stayed, it wouldn't make a difference. She would still go to Tanner. She would still share his bed because her body wouldn't allow it any other way. She wanted him so much that her skin was practically humming with anticipation of his touch.

So there was no reason to have her grandfather remain, just so he could watch her make a fool of herself. Besides, she wouldn't let him put his life on hold.

"No thanks, Pop," she said, threading her arm through his and giving it a squeeze. "I appreciate the offer, but there's a brand-new nursery waiting for you in Florida. Mom needs your help."

"And you don't?"

"I'll always need you, Pop," she said and tipped her head to rest it on his shoulder. "But I've got to stand on my own. This is my mess and I'll either straighten it out or sink. One or the other."

"My money's on you, kid," he told her and patted her hand. "Now, why don't we go and take another look at the new plantings. Want to make sure everything's in good shape before Tom Howard takes me to the airport tomorrow afternoon."

"I can take you, you know. You don't have to get one of your friends to make the drive."

"We've been over that, too," Mike told her with a shake of his head. "Tom's going into

Sacramento to visit his son. There's no reason for you to make the trip. Especially," he added slyly, "when there's plenty going on right here."

He was right, Ivy thought, walking with him through the rows of trees, headed for the back half of the farm. There was plenty going on. And a lot of it was *inside* her. Ivy wasn't at all sure she was doing the right thing by getting even more involved with a man she was lying to. She only knew she couldn't seem to help herself.

It had been too long since she'd been touched. Wanted. Desired. And it felt good to have a man's hands on her again.

But that wasn't entirely true either, she told herself firmly. It wasn't just any man's hands she wanted on her. It was Tanner's. Her heart was falling for him and she couldn't seem to stop that, either. Even knowing as she fell that eventually, her heart would break, as it had once before. Only this time, she thought, the pain was going to be even more deeply felt. How could it not be, when everything else about her time with Tanner was richer, deeper, more profound than anything she'd ever known before?

She glanced over her shoulder at the roofline of Tanner's house. She imagined him in that glass and wood mansion, waiting for her.

And her body burned.

Three hours later, the burning had only intensified.

As if the entire world was collaborating against her, Ivy hadn't been able to get away from the farm any earlier. Was it a karmic warning system? she wondered. Was someone, somewhere trying to tell her something? Trying to get her to step away from Tanner before it was too late?

Because if they were, she wasn't listening. She shivered a little as she climbed the front steps to his porch. In fact, she was actively shutting down her own early warning systems. She didn't want to think. Didn't want to wonder or worry. What she wanted was sex. Mind-blowing, soul-searing sex. And she wasn't leaving here without it.

Her conscience screamed at her that she should tell Tanner the truth. Tell him that she'd been lying to him. She should confess that *she* owned Angel Tree Christmas Farm and tell him all about her plan to soften him up so he'd stop causing trouble.

But, she argued with herself, if the did that, confessed all, then instead of an amazing night filled with what she hoped would be great sex and multiple orgasms…what she'd get would be an argument. Lots of shouting and hurt feelings and—no. She'd tell him the truth eventually. But she wanted this night with him first.

Adjusting the collar of her white cotton blouse, she flipped her hair back out of her face and then wiped her damp palms on the thighs of her best jeans. Not exactly seductive outerwear, she supposed, but she was who she was. And Tanner hadn't seemed put off by her jeans and T-shirt earlier.

Her blood pumped a little faster at the memory

of those two quick stolen orgasms. She wanted more. Wanted to feel him touch her all over. Wanted the warm slide of his skin against hers. She squirmed uncomfortably as liquid heat pooled at her center. Even the fabric of her jeans pressing against her was nearly torture.

She looked over her shoulder at the sunset staining the sky, and the roof of her home. If she had any sense at all, she'd turn around now, go back to her own bedroom and lock the door behind her.

Ivy took a breath, held it, then let it slowly sift from her lungs. She was hoping for control. Hoping for calm. What she got was a whiff of his scent as he quietly opened the front door.

Her head whipped around and her mouth went dry.

His black hair was thick and damp from a shower. His eyes smoldered with the promise of exactly what she needed so desperately. His broad—as she'd guessed—muscular chest was bare and a sprinkling of dark hair dusted his skin, then trailed down across his abdomen to disappear beneath his jeans. The top button of those jeans was unbuttoned, giving her a peek of paler skin and his bare feet were braced wide apart.

He looked her up and down quickly and Ivy was pretty sure she could actually *feel* flames licking at her skin under the intensity of his gaze.

"What took you so long?" he growled in a voice that was low and barely restrained.

She took another short breath and whispered, "Does it matter, now?"

"Nope." He grabbed her hand, tugged her into the house and slammed the door behind her. In seconds, his fingers were undoing the buttons on her shirt. He threw the garment to the floor as she swayed into him.

Ivy lifted her hands and slid them over his chest, loving the feel of his warm, smooth skin beneath her palms. Her thumbs flicked across his flat nipples and he hissed in a breath as he made quick work of the front clasp of her bra. When he slid the straps down her arms to let the damn thing fall on the floor, he filled his hands with her breasts and Ivy groaned aloud.

"I've been wanting you to do that all day," she admitted, beyond pride, beyond anything but the overwhelming need for him.

"Baby, I'm just getting started," he said, then shifted his hands to the waistband of her jeans.

Ivy was way ahead of him. She toed off her sandals and then wriggled in place to get rid of the denim that was separating her from him. Now only her pale pink panties stood between her and Tanner—when he tore them from her, she could only be grateful.

"Oh yeah, this is how I've wanted you for days," he murmured, dipping his head to kiss her, once, twice. His teeth and lips tugged at her mouth and delicious sensations spiraled through her in response. Her entire body was sizzling. She wouldn't have been surprised to glance down and see that she was actually giving off sparks.

"Well, you've got me now," she said and

linked her arms around his neck, going up on her toes so that she could kiss him back more forcefully.

"Damn straight," he said, undoing the buttons of his jeans to allow his really impressive erection to spring forth.

Ivy's stomach did a slow dip and roll and the dampness at her core increased. He was bigger there than David had been. She wasn't a virgin, but she wasn't exactly the most experienced woman on the planet, either. She'd only had one lover and that had been the man she had planned to marry.

Well, there was no marriage in sight here, she told herself as she looked from Tanner's hard, all-too-eager flesh up to his eyes again. But she wasn't looking for that anymore, either. What she needed from him was more basic. More primal.

She was here and she wasn't going to second-guess herself. She and Tanner had been heading toward this moment since the first day she'd stepped inside this house. She knew that without a doubt. There was an attraction between them. A fundamental link that pulled them toward each other even when reason should have kept them apart.

And she wouldn't argue with it. Not today.

Reaching for him, she closed her hand around the thickness of him and watched as he closed his eyes and drew in one long, deep breath. She was more than ready for this. More than impatient to feel him inside her. When she stroked him and slid her fingertips across the sensitive tip of him, he stopped her, and shook his head. "Just a minute."

He reached into his pocket, grabbed a condom and tore it open. She smiled. In her hunger and hurry, she'd tossed caution out the window along with good sense. Thank heaven Tanner was still conscious enough to do the right thing.

When he'd sheathed himself, he looked into her eyes, gave her a slow grin and then set both hands at her waist. Lifting her off her feet, he ordered, "Hook your legs behind my back."

She locked her gaze with his and did just as he'd ordered.

His big hands cupped her bottom and kneaded her soft flesh with an urgent tenderness that sent ripples of expectation rolling through her. "Tanner…"

"Right there with you, baby," he murmured, his eyes staring directly into hers.

She read the same wild, raw desire in his eyes that she knew was written in her own. She struggled for air as an invisible iron band tightened around her chest. She held on to his shoulders and gasped as he pushed himself into her body in one sure thrust. She gasped at the intimate invasion. It had been a long time for her and her body had to adjust to his presence. She settled herself more firmly over him and quickly felt tingles of appreciation light up inside her.

Ivy moved on him then, and her eyes slid shut on a groan as she twisted her hips, reveling in the thick fullness within her. Impaled on his body, she opened her eyes again to meet his. As he moved her up and down on his length, their gazes remained fixed, as if neither of them could bear to break the intimate connections binding them together.

She felt him shudder and watched a muscle in his jaw twitch as he fought for control. She smiled to herself as she silently admitted that she didn't want him controlled. She wanted him wild, abandoned. So she took his mouth with hers, tangling her tongue with his, giving him her breath and greedily taking his for her own. She lowered one hand to stroke his flat nipple with the edge of her thumb and when he groaned into her mouth, she knew she'd won.

He spun around abruptly, braced her back against the door and with his mouth still fused to hers, took her in just the way she wanted. Over and over again, he plunged in and out of her body with a soul shaking rhythm. Each thrust was harder, deeper, than the one before, until all that mattered was the next one and the next. Her mind splintered of thoughts beyond the all-consuming need to reach the pinnacle she was racing toward.

She cupped his face in her hands and kissed him hungrily as his body lay siege to hers. Tension coiled and tightened inside her as she strained for the release she knew was just out of reach. At last, when she thought she might die from the pleasure, a blinding orgasm crashed down on top of her.

Ivy tore her mouth from his and shouted his name as a flood of incredible sensations raced through her with the force of an explosion. And moments later, as the last of the ripples wound through her, Tanner buried his face in the curve of her neck, groaned her name aloud and emptied himself, shuddering in her arms until they were both trembling and clinging to each other for support.

Seconds, then minutes ticked past and still they stood there, braced against a door, each of them too shaken by what had happened to try to move.

Heart hammering in her chest, Ivy absently listened to the mingled sounds of their harsh breathing. When she thought she could speak without her voice breaking, she whispered on a strained chuckle, "Tanner King, you're a man of many talents."

"Ivy Holloway," he managed to say before he lifted his head to meet her eyes, "you ain't seen nothin' yet."

Eight

He carried her upstairs to the bedroom.

Ivy smiled up at him and Tanner felt like a damn superhero for carrying her. The truth was, he didn't want to let go of her long enough for her to climb the stairs on her own.

He'd had her once, hard and fast and it had only fed the quickening fires inside him. Now he wanted to see his fantasy in the flesh, so to speak. He wanted to stretch her out, naked, across his bed. Then he wanted to take his time and lick his way up and down her amazing body.

Instantly, he was hard again and wishing he'd just peeled his jeans off downstairs. The walk down the long, dimly lit hallways seemed to take forever. But soon enough, he was kicking his bedroom door open and stalking across the room.

The heavy, bloodred quilt was pulled back already, displaying fresh white sheets. A dozen pillows were mounded against the headboard and the last glow of the sunset painted the sky outside the window a deep orange. One bedside lamp was turned on, creating a golden puddle of light and when Tanner laid her down on the bed, her bare skin seemed to glow in its radiance.

She stretched her arms up over her head and sighed as she wriggled against the mattress. "I feel wonderful," she told him.

"You're about to feel even better," he said.

"Promises, promises," she teased and held her arms out for him.

Tanner shook his head slowly, tore off his jeans and grabbed a fresh condom from the bedside table. He sheathed himself again and noticed that her gaze was locked on the motion. Instantly, he went even harder and he wouldn't have thought that possible. It seemed though, that where Ivy was concerned, his body couldn't get enough.

"Tanner, come to me," she coaxed.

"In time," he said and went down on his knees beside the bed. Grabbing hold of her, he pulled her to the edge of the mattress and draped her legs over his shoulders.

"Oh, Tanner…" She pushed up on her elbows to look at him and she was still watching him when he first tasted her. She gasped aloud and moved against his mouth.

He ran his tongue along her slick folds and tasted her as if she were running with honey. Her scent flooded him and Tanner gave himself up to the fantasy of having her at his mercy, naked and writhing.

Again and again, his lips, tongue and teeth worked her most sensitive flesh. The only sounds in the room were the sighs of her breathing and the slapping of her hands against the mattress as she fought for something to hold on to.

He relished her and when he felt her coiling for release, her body tightening, he stopped, pulled back and grinned at her outraged squeak of "Don't stop now!"

She was shaking with unanswered need and Tanner skimmed the tips of his fingers across her center. She jolted and then settled down again, waiting breathlessly for him to finish what he'd started. And when he couldn't wait another moment, he did just that. He flicked his tongue across the one spot that held so many sensations and then he suckled her as she splintered in his grasp, crying his name.

When her climax at last ended, he rose up, joined her on the bed and rolled her over onto her stomach. She sighed blissfully as his hands rubbed up and down the length of her spine, tracing every curve, every line of her body. His mouth went next and he licked and kissed his way across her skin until he knew her body as well as he did his own.

She squirmed against him, rubbing her bottom into him and the fires inside him roared.

"Again," he muttered thickly. "I need you again. Now."

"Now," she agreed and when he pulled her up to her knees, she threw her hair out of her face and looked back over her shoulder at him. "Be in me, Tanner. Be with me."

"Grab hold of the headboard," he said and moved to cover her body with his. When she had a grip on the intricately carved oak wood, Tanner held her hips still and entered her to the hilt. He buried himself as deeply as he could and knew it would never be deep enough.

He loved the feel of her hot, slick flesh surrounding his. He groaned at the perfection of the moment and gave himself over to the demands of his body. She moved with him, into him, her soft gasps and heavy sighs creating a sort of music that sent his own blood into a dizzying dance.

With every stroke, he claimed her. With every touch, he adored her. With every breath, he hungered for her. He felt her climax shudder through her and before the last of it had died away, he joined her and the two of them fell into a scatter of stars.

Three hours later, Ivy turned her head on the pillow and looked at the man lying next to her. They'd come together again and again as if neither of them could bear the idea of being apart even momentarily. She'd never experienced anything like what Tanner made her feel. Just looking at him turned her heart over in her chest and she realized with a jolt that she was falling in love with him. Ivy bit back a groan and closed her eyes briefly. How had this happened? She hadn't wanted this. Hadn't expected it. Hadn't been looking for it.

And now that she'd found it she wasn't entirely sure how to handle it. The problem here was, when Tanner had been just a neighbor—a potential friend—a small white lie hadn't seemed like such a big deal. Now though, she knew that everything had changed. What she felt for

Tanner was so much bigger than what she and David had shared, she almost felt guilty admitting it to herself. But it was true and the other undeniable truth was, when Tanner found out she'd been lying to him, this relationship would be over.

She didn't want it to be over.

Idly, she wondered what might have happened if Tanner hadn't had the foresight to have a condom handy. Lost in the throes of a passion she'd never known before, Ivy had completely disregarded the need for protection. If Tanner had forgotten too, might they have made a baby tonight? And what then? If they had, would she allow a lie to remain between them?

"What're you thinking?" he asked quietly.

She came up out of her thoughts and pushed them all to the back of her mind. Worries for another day. Another time. Right now, she didn't want to risk spoiling what they had.

"Nothing, really."

"You looked pretty somber for nothing." He

went up on his elbow and reached out with his free hand to rub her shoulder.

Just that simple touch was enough to stir her up again and she wouldn't have thought that was possible. Would it always be that explosive between them? Would she forever erupt into passion so easily around him?

Would she get the chance to find out?

She took a breath and gave him a small piece of the larger truth.

"I was just thinking I was grateful that you'd had the presence of mind to remember a condom," she said, then admitted, "I wasn't thinking very clearly at the time."

His features tightened. "You should. No kid deserves to be an accident."

The words came so fast and harsh, it stole her breath from her. There was pain glittering in his eyes and the rigidity of his jaw told her that she'd inadvertently struck a nerve. Carefully, she tried to smooth things over. "If I were to get pregnant, I'd never consider my child a mistake, Tanner."

"Maybe not," he allowed, his gaze locked with hers. "But others would. Have."

There was a chill in his voice now, to match the darkness in his eyes.

He pushed one hand through his hair and shook his head as if disgusted with himself for opening this conversation. "All I meant was, I don't make bastards," he said simply. "That's my father's thing."

The casual use of the ugly word jabbed at her. His beautiful eyes were shuttered as if sealing her out. There was old pain there, she caught just a glimpse of it before he disguised it behind a layer of nonchalance. "Tanner..."

"Please," he said on a sharp laugh. "I don't need sympathy. I grew up fine. I've got more half brothers and cousins than anyone should have. I'm only saying that I'm careful."

He brushed aside her concern and she understood the need to cling to your own pride so she wouldn't offer him compassion when he clearly didn't want it. But she also wouldn't let him back away from a subject that obviously needed to be spoken about. "I get that. But there's more, isn't there?"

"What's that supposed to mean?"

It meant that she was beginning to see why Tanner was so closed off from people. He'd had a lonely childhood despite what he was saying and the memories, if not the hurts of it, were still vividly with him.

"Well," she said softly, "How you feel about Christmas for instance."

"I don't need therapy."

"Good. Not a therapist."

He glared at her. "Then drop it."

"What is it about Christmas that you hate, Tanner?"

His jaw worked as if he were biting back a flood of words trying to escape. Lamplight shone on his tanned skin and made him seem golden. And though she could stretch out one hand to touch him, Ivy knew he was farther from her than he'd ever been.

A tense moment or two passed before finally, he shrugged and said, "I never really did Christmas as a kid." He shifted position and sat up, resting against pillows he bunched against the headboard, sheet pooled across his abdomen.

"That's not the only reason," she said.

He gave her a quick look. "Why do you care, Ivy?"

"Call it curiosity," she told him, though it was more. So much more. She wanted to understand him. Wanted to *know* him.

Shaking his head, he said, "Okay, doesn't matter anyway. My holidays were usually spent in an empty hotel room wondering when my mom was going to come back. She was usually off lining up her next lover and didn't have time to do the tree and present thing." He shrugged as if what he was saying meant nothing, though she could see it did. "My nanny usually got me something so it wasn't a complete wash. And whatever my dad sent me always arrived around the twenty-fifth, so it didn't matter really."

A twinge of pity zipped through her. Not for the man he was now, but for the boy he'd once been. On the outside, looking in and not knowing why. The boy had been alone and miserable. The man was still alone, yet had convinced himself that it was the way he wanted it.

"I can see in your eyes that you're getting all weepy on my account," he said and shook his head with a smile. "You don't have to. I did fine. I *do* fine."

She took a breath and blew it out. "Of course you do. But I don't mind telling you I'd like to step back in time and shake your mother until her teeth rattled."

He laughed a little and she was grateful to see some of the tension leave his features.

"You know," Ivy told him quietly, "you don't have to avoid Christmas forever. Just because you had crappy holidays as a kid doesn't mean you have to continue the tradition. You can make your own choices instead of living with old hurts."

"Here comes the therapy," he muttered, sliding a look at her. "Everybody's got answers. Everybody knows what somebody else should do. What makes you think I'm in pain over something that happened decades ago? What makes you so sure that I'm suffering? I do what I want when I want. I don't need your concern because it's pointless. There is no angry little boy inside me waiting to be soothed, so spare me."

"Wow." She sat up, drawing the sheet with her and clutching it to her chest. All of her earlier warm, fuzzy thoughts were quickly dissipating. Okay yes, she loved him. That didn't mean she was going to sit there and be a target for him. "For a guy who's put it all behind him, you sound a little sensitive on the subject."

"Why shouldn't I be?" he demanded. "Where do you get off giving me advice, anyway? What do you know about pain, Ivy? Easy enough to sit on the sidelines and tell everybody else how they should *get over it* and move on. Well you don't know jack about what my life is like."

"No, I don't," she said, fisting her hand in the fabric of the sheet and squeezing. She wasn't sure how they'd gone from spectacular sex and cozy afterglow to this raging argument, but she wasn't about to let him talk to her like that. "But I know enough to stop licking old wounds. I know that shutting myself away in a house where I never have to speak to anyone isn't the answer."

"Is that right?" His dark eyes went wide as he feigned astonishment. "And you've come by this magical knowledge how? Watching TV? What great pains do you have to deal with? Hell, you live in a town that might as well be Christmas central!"

A sharp jab of hurt bit into her and Ivy lifted her chin to glare at him. She knew what this was, damn it—why they were having this ridiculous fight. They were both feeling emotionally shaken by what they'd shared and they were both going into defense mode. Oh, wasn't that wonderful, she thought. And just when had she gotten so insightful, anyway?

"Fine," she said, scooting off the bed because she needed to be standing on her own two feet, not sharing the mattress with a man she wanted to kick, "you don't want advice, your choice. But don't bother to assume that you're the only person on the planet who's had trouble."

"Ivy—"

"No," she stopped him, thoroughly disgusted with him now. "You said you had a mother and father. Are they still alive?"

"Yeah…"

"My dad died when I was a little girl," she told him. "I miss him still."

A flicker of what might have been regret crossed his face briefly. "Look, maybe I was out of line…"

She tipped her head to one side and stared at him. "Have you ever loved anyone, Tanner? I mean *love?*"

His gaze darkened. "No."

"Well, I have."

He blinked but that was the only sign of surprise he showed her. She didn't care. All she wanted to do now was get out of this house and away from him. But she wasn't going anywhere until she'd clued him in on a little something.

"Four years ago, my fiancé David was in a car accident and died."

"Damn it, Ivy…" He came up off the bed and made to go to her, but she scrambled back and away, holding up one hand to keep him at bay.

"Three weeks before our wedding," she said, "I went to David's funeral." Tears blurred her vision, but she blinked them back. Somehow they'd both torn open old wounds and were now taking turns dribbling salt on them. All to avoid talking about the emotional connection they'd made. She didn't know who she was more furious with. Tanner? Or herself?

The only way out now was to keep on going. "I could have curled up in a ball and reveled in the pain," she whispered. "I could have shut myself up in the house and never talked to anyone again. But you know what, Tanner? That's not life. That's just taking up space. So you keep going forward. You don't stay trapped in the past, you move on. You keep breathing because that's what life is."

Her breath was hitching in her chest and she

felt the tears clogging her throat now, too. Damn it, she didn't want to cry in front of him. That would just put a capper on this scene, wouldn't it?

"Ivy, I didn't know."

"No, you didn't," she muttered, heading for the open bedroom door. "And I wasn't looking for sympathy either, Tanner, so spare me that."

He grabbed his jeans, tugged them on and followed her when she swept from the room like a queen dragging her sheet cape behind her.

"Damn it, Ivy, don't go."

"There's no reason to stay," she told him, gathering up her clothes and dressing as hurriedly as she possibly could.

He grabbed her arm, but she pulled free. "I don't much like you right now, Tanner, so I'm going home."

"This is my fault?"

She tossed her hair out of her eyes and stepped into her sandals. "It's not about *fault,* Tanner. It's about this going really wrong really fast and now I need to leave."

"Who's hiding now?" he asked.

She stilled, lifted her gaze to his and gave him a sad smile. "Touché, Tanner. Nice shot. Now just…shut up."

Before he could stop her, she threw the front door open and was stalking down the steps. He watched her go and wished he could rewrite time. If he could, he'd have avoided the argument entirely. They'd still be upstairs, in his bed. Instead, he was standing alone in the dark.

When she arrived the next afternoon for work, Tanner was waiting for her in the hallway. He'd done a lot of thinking the night before and it had occurred to him that he knew how to fix what had gone wrong between them. So he'd gotten up early, driven to Lake Tahoe to do some shopping and now he was back, prepared to accept her thanks. Then he'd take her upstairs again and remind her why they were so good together.

"Tanner." Ivy stopped just inside the doorway and looked up at him.

He saw the shadows beneath her eyes and

knew she'd spent the night as sleepless as he'd been. Somehow that made him feel better. And he was more sure than ever that he was about to end the stalemate between them.

"Ivy, I did some thinking," he said.

"Yeah, me too," she said and scrubbed both hands across her face. "I really think we should talk, Tanner. I need to—"

"Do me a favor?" he asked, bringing the package he'd been holding behind his back forward. The white box was long and narrow and wrapped with a string of red ribbon. "Open this first."

"What? Why?"

He lifted one shoulder. "Does it matter? Just open it."

She took the box from him, shot him another curious glance and then pulled the ribbon free. When she opened the box, she blew out a breath and whispered, "It's lovely."

"I wanted you to have it," he said, glad that she liked the diamond-encrusted white gold watch.

"Why did you buy it for me?" she asked and her voice was soft, curious.

"I wanted you to have it."

"Because of last night."

"Well," he said, *"yeah."*

She snapped the box closed and handed it back to him. "No, thank you."

"What?"

"I don't want the watch, Tanner," she said and now she sounded tired. "I'm not interested in your money or your presents. If you're sorry for last night, just say so."

He opened his mouth then closed it again. Tanner didn't do apologies. When he had a regret, he gifted his way out of it. He'd learned early and well from his mother that the way to win a woman's forgiveness was with shiny presents. And, he told himself in disgust, it had always worked for him before. *Trust Ivy to be different.*

"You can't do it, can you?" she whispered, shaking her head. "You can't bring yourself to say you're sorry."

His hand fisted around the jewelry box as irritation swept him. This wasn't going at all as he'd planned. Damn it, why did she have to be so difficult? Why couldn't she just accept his gift and let it go?

"It's just a gift, Ivy," he said tightly.

"No, it's not," she argued. "It's a bribe."

"Excuse me?"

"It's saying *accept this and stop being mad.* Well, forget it, Tanner. I'm still angry and a pretty watch isn't going to change that."

"What the hell do you want from me?" he de-manded.

"Too much," she said, then brushed past him on her way to the kitchen. "Now, I've got a lot to do, so I'm going to work."

He stared down at his rejected offering and wondered where he'd gone so wrong. Since the moment he met her, Ivy had been like no other woman he'd ever known. What had made him think she'd allow herself to be bought off by trinkets? He looked off down the hall toward the kitchen, and told himself that for the first time in his life, he was completely out of his depths with a woman.

He didn't have a clue what to do next.

Nine

For the next couple of days, Ivy tried to stay as far from Tanner as possible. Not an easy task, considering she spent a few hours each day at his house. Even worse, all she could do was think about their night together. What she'd found in his arms, what he'd made her feel.

She was on a tightrope—trying to keep her balance in a situation that was designed to splinter her equilibrium. She wanted him and couldn't have him. Wanted to tell him the truth and had to keep lying. Wanted to quit but couldn't bear the thought of leaving.

How in the world had her life gotten so complicated?

Oh, she never should have slept with him. She'd known at the time that it was a mistake of giant proportions. But instead of thinking with her head, she'd let her too-hungry body lead her down a road that was going to go nowhere but misery.

What she should have done was quit her job. She knew that.

Or, tell him the truth and let him fire her.

In fact, she had made up her mind to be honest with him and tell him everything, that morning she'd arrived to find he'd bought her a diamond watch of all things. Imagine him thinking that she'd want the stupid watch in the first place— sure, he didn't know she was a farmer, but how many housekeepers did he know who wore diamonds?

"Idiot," she muttered, taking a pot roast out of the oven and setting it on a cooling rack on the counter.

Was *I'm sorry* so far out of his lexicon that

he couldn't even imagine saying it? Instead he'd had to drive at least two hours to go shopping only to turn around and come back? Was buying something that much easier than apologizing?

Oh, she supposed he'd meant well enough, remembering now the expectant expression on his face as he had watched her open his gift. He'd no doubt assumed that once she caught sight of the shiny bauble, all would be forgiven and she'd fling herself into his arms.

She didn't know whether to be amused or sorry for him.

Did he really believe all he had to do was toss diamonds at her and she'd be happy as a clam again? How could he think it would be that easy? That she could be bought? Had every woman in his life been so cheaply acquired? Well, if they had, then he was in for a rude awakening when it came to Ivy Angel Holloway.

But even as she thought that, she realized that maybe he didn't care. He'd been avoiding her as strictly as she had him for the last couple of days. She'd heard him typing or muttering from behind the closed door of his office. But he hadn't spoken to her since she'd handed him back the watch.

So where did that leave her?

"You know exactly where," she whispered. "You're in love with a man who doesn't even know who you really are."

A scratching at the back door caught her attention and Ivy gratefully shut down her self-pity party to check it out. She opened the door to a cool night, with a sharp wind racing through the trees and found a bedraggled dog staring up at her through huge, limpid brown eyes. One ear stood straight up, the other flopped over his head. His fur was matted over a well-defined rib cage telling Ivy that he hadn't eaten in quite a while. He wasn't wearing a collar, but he was sitting politely on the porch, watching her hopefully.

In a quiet, soothing tone, she asked, "Well now, who are you?"

The dog's tail whipped back and forth across

the porch and he regally lifted one paw as an offering.

Charmed, in spite of the dog's straggly appearance, she reached out carefully to gently hold his paw before stroking the top of his head. He leaned into her touch as if hungry for the connection and Ivy's heart melted.

"Poor baby. How long have you been on your own?"

Even as compassion swelled inside her for the poor little thing, anger blistered the edges of her heart as she realized just what had happened to this dog. She knew all too well that sometimes people from the city drove through the area and abandoned pets they could no longer keep for whatever reasons. It infuriated her that anyone could be so callous as to just drive away from what had been a member of their family. But she'd seen it too often to be surprised by the action.

"Bet you're hungry, as well as lonely, aren't you?"

The dog whined a little and she turned for the

kitchen, intending to get him food and water. She stopped abruptly when she ran into Tanner standing just behind her. She shrieked, then clapped one hand to her chest. "Seriously? You need to not do that to people. I'm going to have a heart attack before I'm thirty if you keep that up."

"What is that?" he asked, looking past her to the dog.

"It's a dog."

He grimaced at her. "I know that. What's it doing here?"

"Looking for food," she said, with a glance back at the poor creature now staring up at Tanner. "And some company."

"That's probably the dog that's been leaving his calling card on my lawn," he muttered.

"Probably," she agreed, and moved to stroke the dog's head again, as if to make up to him for Tanner's surly attitude. But the animal wasn't interested in her attentions now. Instead, he stood up and walked straight to Tanner, then sat down again, placing one paw atop Tanner's foot.

Typical of animals, it went directly to the one person who was less than happy to see it. Ivy couldn't help smiling, despite the fact that she didn't think the little dog was going to get much of a welcome reception.

She knew how it felt. There was no shining warmth in Tanner's gaze for her, either. But then, they'd spent the last couple of days studiously avoiding each other, so what did she really expect? Shaking her head to dislodge the wayward thoughts, she focused instead on the dog and the man staring down at it.

"He likes you," she said.

"He's filthy."

"And starving, no doubt," she added, moving past the duo staring at each other with mixed looks of suspicion and curiosity. "His family must have dumped him here at least a week ago. Looks like he hasn't eaten in days."

"Dumped him?" Tanner asked, shooting her a look. "What?"

She dug around in a cupboard for two bowls. One she filled with fresh water and the other she carried to the counter. Shaving off a couple of generous slices of the freshly cooked pot roast, she broke them up in the bowl and then carried both offerings to the dog.

The animal glanced at them, but wouldn't tear his gaze from Tanner to eat, regardless of the fact that he had to be desperate for food.

Ivy shook her head as she watched the little guy. He was no bigger than a medium-sized spaniel, but he looked even smaller thanks to the fact that he'd been scrounging for survival on his own. He must have been terrified, she thought sadly. New sights, new sounds, nothing familiar and no pack to turn to.

"City people," she whispered with a shake of her head. "They drive out to the countryside and dump whatever pet they no longer want along the roadside. Then they take off again, leaving behind a poor animal who has no idea how to survive on its own."

"What the hell kind of people would do that?"

She smiled at him, pleased that he was as

outraged by the practice as she was. "You'd be surprised."

"Don't know why I would be," he muttered, going down on one knee to study the dog more closely. "Mostly, people suck."

"On this one point, I'll agree."

He flashed her a smile, then turned back to the dog.

Tentatively, he rubbed the animal's head and smiled as the dog whined a little in appreciation of the affection. Then Tanner scooted the food bowl closer to him and watched as the animal politely ate what he'd been given instead of wolfing it down in huge, starved gulps.

"So, what am I supposed to do with him?" Tanner mused, reaching out to pet the dog again.

"You could call the pound," she suggested, almost as a challenge, to see what his reaction would be. He didn't disappoint her.

"The *pound?*" He looked at her in astonishment. "Won't they just put him down?"

Pleased at his response, Ivy said, "If he's not

adopted, then after a week or so, yeah, they would."

"Well screw that."

Ivy smiled to herself. She'd been wondering how the two of them would ever start speaking to each other again after they'd left everything so muddled and confused between them. Then this little dog had appeared and in their shared concern, that last night together was, if not forgotten, then at least set aside. For now.

She'd have to be honest with him eventually, tell him who she was and then she'd have to live with the knowledge that anything they might have had together was ended. But that was for another day.

Tanner King might not be very fond of people, she thought. But, as she watched him with the dog, she knew that he had a full and generous heart, no matter how he might pretend otherwise.

"Okay then," she offered, "if you're going to keep him, then we should take him to the vet and get him checked out. And buy him a leash and a collar."

He shook his head slowly as the dog finished his meal and turned to Tanner, leaning up against him with a heavy sigh of relief at having been found and accepted. Laughing, Tanner said, "And shampoo. Definitely shampoo."

The dog sighed with contentment again and stretched out on the kitchen floor, completely at home.

Tanner waited until just before Ivy was leaving for home to say, "Thanks. For helping with the dog. He probably hasn't slept in a week. He's practically unconscious."

"He likes his new bed then?"

Tanner grimaced. "No. He likes *my* bed. Anyway, thanks."

"You're welcome." She hitched her shoulder bag higher and looked at him.

Weren't they being polite?

He hated that things were so strained between them. He hated that their incredible night together had ended so abruptly. Mostly, though he hated that they hadn't repeated it. Just having her here in the house, Tanner's body was taut and ready all the damn time. Now that he'd had her, the desire he'd felt, rather than being sated had only been enhanced. Now he knew what she felt like, tasted like and he wanted her again and again.

Hell, he could hardly draw a breath without inhaling her scent—real or imagined. His dreams were filled with her and every waking moment was a study in torture. He had to find a way to get her back into his bed.

"About the other night," he said.

"I know," she said softly. "It was a mistake."

He jolted. "A mistake?"

"God, yes," she breathed. "It never should have happened, Tanner. It just makes everything so… complicated."

That's what he'd thought at first, too. That's why he'd bought her the stupid watch. But it wasn't. The mistake, he thought, was not making love to her again. "Doesn't have to be," he said, "it's only complicated if we make it that way. If we just take it for what it is—"

She looked up at him and in the bright kitchen light, her eyes looked impossibly pure and deep. "Which is what?"

Her features were wary, and there was a shadow of regret in those beautiful eyes of hers. He didn't know what she was thinking. How the hell could he? He knew what he wanted though. Now all he had to do was convince her that he was right.

"It's two adults who want each other. Why does it have to be more than that?"

She laughed sadly and shook her head. "Because it's not enough. Not for me."

"It could be."

"I don't want it to be," she countered quickly, then reached out to lay one hand on his forearm.

Heat skittered along his skin and Tanner sucked in a deep breath to calm the suddenly raging sense of need clawing at his insides. He took her hand in his and stroked his thumb across her knuckles until he saw her shiver in response.

He should have expected this. Ivy Holloway was not his usual kind of woman. She was home and hearth. She was the forever kind of woman, not the pick-her-up-at-a-club-and-forget-her-the-next-day type. Which meant Tanner was out of his element completely. He didn't do forever. Hell, he barely did months.

But he wanted her in a way he'd never wanted anyone else. So who could blame him for trying to convince her to step out of her comfort zone and try something different.

"Why the hell not, Ivy?" He drew her in closer, needing to feel her in the circle of his arms. Her breasts pillowed against his chest and he wanted her more than his next breath. "We were good together. *Great.*"

"Yeah, we really were," she said, swallowing hard as if she, too, were feeling the swamping flood of heat that was roaring through him. "That night was…really fabulous, Tanner. I mean that. But I'm just not the *fling* kind of girl, you know? Besides, there are other reasons why this should not be happening."

He caught her scent and thought nothing in the world had ever smelled better than whatever the hell it was she used to wash her hair. Everything in him was hard and tight and desperate to hold onto her. He didn't know what she was talking about, but as far as he was concerned, there was no good reason for turning your back on what they'd found together.

"I didn't say this was a fling. Who says that anymore?" He gave her a slow smile filled with the promises of what he'd like to be doing to her at the moment instead of talking. When she didn't respond, he said, "Fine. So I'm not talking about forever, but there's no reason you have to label this—whatever we have—as a fling. I'm talking about now, Ivy. What we feel. What we want. What we could be to each other."

"Yeah," she said with a laugh that had no humor in it. "I get that. And that's why I can't. One of the reasons, anyway."

"Give me another." He ran his hands up and

down her back and felt her move languorously beneath his touch.

"I work for you?"

"I could fire you."

"You probably should," she whispered.

"What?"

"Nothing," she said and reluctantly stepped back out of his embrace. Turning her face up to his, she said, "I really can't, Tanner. Trust me when I say one day you'll understand."

He didn't know what was going on with her, but damned if Tanner could ever remember a time in his life when he'd had a woman turn him down so neatly. Along with taking a ding out of what some considered his too healthy ego, her rejection slapped at what he was feeling for her. Because if she was trying to pretend she wasn't as turned on as he was, she was a liar.

"That's bull, Ivy. I know what you're feeling. I know you want me just as badly as I want you."

"I really do…"

"Then what's the problem?"

"Tanner…"

"Look, if you've got something to say to me, say it now."

"I should," she said with a short nod. "I really should. But I'm not going to, because apparently, I'm a coward. Good night, Tanner."

She left and he stood alone in the brightly lit kitchen watching her disappear into the darkness.

"You're impossible, you know that, right?" Ivy shook her head as she stepped into the kitchen the following day.

"Can't fault a guy for trying," Tanner told her, watching her reaction as she looked around the room.

The watch hadn't worked. He knew that, though he still wasn't entirely sure why not. An expensive watch would have swayed not only his mother, but every other woman he'd ever known in a heartbeat. Ivy, though, was a whole different story. So he'd tried to keep that in mind when he set up this little surprise.

The dog barked and jumped at her in excitement, as if even he knew something special was going on.

Ivy turned in a slow circle, letting her gaze slide across the kitchen as she did so. Every surface was covered in flowers. He'd bought out Carol Sands' shop, forcing her to close for the rest of the day to make a trip into the city to stock up fresh.

There were vases and bowls filled with roses and daisies and some kind of weird purple flower. There were ivy plants and orchids and even a few tulips. The scent in the room was overwhelming and the brilliant splashes of color were a feast for the eyes.

But all he had eyes for was Ivy.

"You like?"

She smiled and looked at him. "I'd be crazy *not* to like," she pointed out. "But Tanner, you don't have to make a big statement like this."

He shoved both hands into his pockets and shrugged. "I saw your reaction to the watch, believe me, I know. At least, I'm learning."

Ivy winced and walked toward him, trailing her fingertips across a dark peach rose. "I'm sorry, Tanner. But when you gave me that watch as if you expected it to buy your way out of an argument…"

"It always has before," he told her, not ashamed to admit that he'd fallen back on tried-and-true in an attempt to heal the breach with her.

She shook her head again and smiled wryly. "What am I supposed to do with you?"

"I can think of a few things," he said, reaching for her.

But Ivy stepped back, preventing his touch. "It wouldn't solve anything, Tanner. Don't you see that?"

"What's to solve? I want you. You want me. End of story."

"I wish it were that simple."

"It could be. You're making this harder than it has to be."

"And now we're having the same argument all over again."

They were and that hadn't been his intention

at all. There was only one thing left to do. To say. "Ivy, I'm…sorry."

She blinked at him, clearly surprised. Well, she wasn't the only one. He couldn't even remember the last time he'd apologized to anyone. But as he'd already acknowledged, Ivy was different.

"Whatever's going on between us, I want to fix it."

Reaching up to cup his jaw briefly in the palm of her hand, she whispered, "Oh, Tanner. I don't know if we can."

Over the next few days, the tension between Ivy and Tanner only escalated. Neither of them broached the subject that seemed to hover over them. Ivy did her job, but there were no more shared moments while Tanner worked on his next project. She steered clear of him and he missed her interference.

Which only went to prove that he'd been right about hiring her in the first place. And the next time he talked to Mitchell, he was going to tell his old friend that in no uncertain terms. If he'd never let Ivy into his life, then Tanner's world would be just as it always had been. Quiet. Controlled. Orderly.

Well, mostly.

After all, Hairy was a part of his world now, too. And the dog had become such a part of Tanner's routine, he could hardly remember life without the little mutt. A bath had lightened the dog's fur color to a honey gold and a couple of good meals had already started filling him out.

Funny, when he was a kid, all Tanner had wanted was his own dog. Of course, moving from palatial hotel to hotel was no way of life for a dog of the kind he had wanted. A boy's dog, not one of those purebred, prissy types older women and young girls carried around in their purses.

Yet, once he'd grown up and had his own place, he'd never once considered getting a dog for himself. It hadn't seemed important anymore. Now, he couldn't imagine why not.

Tanner and Ivy had taken the dog to the vet to

get his shots and the news that in spite of being malnourished, Hairy was in surprisingly good condition. The vet guessed his age at about three and told Tanner that with love, good food and exercise, he should be perfectly fine in a week or so.

It took far less time than that.

Hairy had taken command of the glass and wood palace that Tanner called home. He slept on the designer couches, or Tanner's bed, had his own food and water bowls in the kitchen and lay at Tanner's feet while he worked. Ivy took him for a walk most every day when she arrived and sometimes, Tanner accompanied them. Those walks were quiet adventures though, since each of them not only refused to speak about what was between them—they also avoided even brushing up against each other. And the banked lust pulsing inside him was threatening to engulf him completely. But the damn woman was more stubborn than he'd have guessed.

She treated him as she would have an acquaintance. Someone she didn't know very well and intended to keep it that way. There were no more easy smiles, no casual touches of her hand to his and no snooping in his office to see what he was creating next. Which was just as well, Tanner told himself since the game he was working on now starred an avenging angel with the face and figure of Ivy Holloway.

He couldn't seem to tear her from his mind any more than he could train his body to not respond to her.

God, he wanted her.

Every time he saw her, he remembered what they'd shared on that one amazing night. But whenever he thought about reawakening the passion between them, something held him back. Maybe it was that last conversation. She'd made it clear enough she wasn't interested in another bout of hot, sweaty sex. And damned if he'd coerce a woman into his bed, for God's sake.

Plus, there was something else.

She'd been damned secretive about why she was turning away from him. He had to wonder why. As much as he desired her, admired her,

Tanner couldn't get past the fact that she was an unknown variable. He liked order in his life for the simple reason that, as a child, his life had been chaos. With rules, order, there was no room for disarray.

No room for pain or betrayal.

But you got a dog, his mind argued.

Hairy was different, he assured himself. A dog learned the rules and mostly kept them. But a woman like Ivy? Hot then cold? He couldn't count on what she'd say or do from one moment to the next. She didn't even believe in rules. Life with Ivy would be nothing *but* disruptions.

He thought about the feel of her skin, the taste of her mouth, the heady sensation of claiming her body with his and told himself that maybe chaos had its place. Then he'd come back to his senses and realize that sex would only cause problems. Better to maintain an even keel. Keep their relationship as platonic as she seemed to want it.

"Probably best all the way around anyway," he muttered.

He just wished he could stop thinking about her every damn minute.

Reaching down to pat the dog, Tanner then leaned back in his office chair and fired off an e-mail to the programmers at his company. He was almost finished with the preliminary sketches of the characters for the new game and as he thought it, he glanced at the woman he'd drawn only that morning. Ivy's face stared back at him from the page. Her eyes, her nose, her mouth, swollen from his kisses. Her image held a flashing sword in the air and the wings that spread from her back were alive with power.

First, she had become Lady Gwen. Now, he mused, she was Aurelia the Avenger.

He was in bad shape.

"Damn it," he muttered, shaking those thoughts and more from his mind. He was starting a new game. Something he usually thrived on. Building characters, creating scenes, devising the ins and outs of the rules to be followed. Rules. Games, like life, needed rules. But Ivy kept shattering his.

He rubbed the back of his neck with one hand and grumbled under his breath. He'd met Nathan's deadline, his company was about to become the hottest thing in computer gaming and still, he was sitting here like he was in mourning.

What the hell was going on?

Why, Tanner wondered, did he feel as if there was something left undone? Something... wrong.

Ivy put the finishing touches on the chocolate cake she'd made for Tanner and told herself that this just couldn't go on. The last few days had been so hard, she simply couldn't let it continue. She had to tell him the truth. Had to get everything out into the open. She was walking around with what felt like two hundred pounds on her shoulders. On her heart.

She just wasn't built for lying.

Her grandfather had been so right, she thought, suddenly wishing Pop were sitting in his favorite chair at home, so she could go and talk this over with him. But he and her mom were both in Florida, happily building the new Angel Nursery. She'd talked to them both a day or so ago and had managed to hide her own misery in the face of their happiness.

She didn't need to worry her family long-distance. Besides, she'd dug this hole for herself, it was going to be up to her to dig her way out. Ivy only wished she knew if Tanner cared for her. Heaven knew the man was so shuttered and closed off, it would take an act of God for him to admit it, but if she could believe those feelings were there, she could live without the words if she had to.

Maybe.

But even if he did care for her, would it last once he knew the truth? From what little he'd told her about himself and his family, she knew that he didn't trust many people. So when she admitted to tricking him deliberately, she couldn't imagine that he'd take it very well.

Understatement.

She groaned and set down the frosting knife.

The last few days had been so hard, being around him and not touching him. Desire flared inside her every time he came anywhere near her. To be so close and yet so far away from him at the same time, tore at her in a way she'd never imagined possible. But it was more than just the wanting, she told herself grimly. It was Tanner himself. Loving him and not being able to tell him so was the hardest thing she'd ever done.

She remembered that last heated conversation and the words she'd said kept haunting her. *I'm a coward.* She hadn't liked the sound of that. Or the way it felt. She'd never run from anything in her life, damn it and she wasn't going to start now.

Ivy had thought this all over for days and she had finally reached a major decision. She was through lying. She was through playing games and keeping secrets. It was no way to live.

She loved Tanner King. After David died, Ivy had never expected to fall in love again, but now that she had, she refused to hide from it.

Refused to chance losing it because she was too afraid to admit that she'd made a mistake.

She'd seen from the first day that Tanner had a trust issue. Why else would he shut himself off from everyone and everything? Work in a small room in his house and never get involved with anyone? It was all about trust. And how could she expect Tanner to trust her when she was lying to him every moment she kept quiet about the truth?

"So, no more lies," she said softly, liking the sound of it. No matter what happened to her and Tanner now, she would at least know that she'd been honest with him.

When her cell phone rang, Ivy was grateful for the respite from her own crazed thoughts. She glanced at the caller ID, then flipped the phone open and said, "Hi Dan, what's up?"

Her farm manager said, "Didn't want to bother you while you were at King's place, but Ivy, there's a problem with the decorative bridge you wanted across the creek in time for the Harrington wedding."

"What?" she asked, barely managing to stifle a groan.

Dan Collins started talking fast and Ivy frowned as his words sunk in. There was a huge wedding scheduled for the coming weekend and everyone at Angel Christmas Tree Farm was working hard to make sure it came off without a hitch. The happy couple was from San Francisco and the bride was the daughter of a very wealthy man.

The wedding was bound to make the society pages of the city's largest newspapers and with that kind of word-of-mouth, Ivy's neophyte wedding business could really take off in a hurry. She couldn't afford to have any mistakes.

"Okay, so you're saying the lumberyard ran out of white cedar?" she repeated. "How is that possible? Having wood available is their job!"

"Well, they're not out, so much as they're behind in their deliveries."

"Great."

"Not too bad," Dan told her. "Most of the

bridge is completed. It's only the railing the crew hasn't finished."

"Yes, but we still have to get it painted and let it dry before the wedding." She rubbed her forehead as a headache began to erupt. "So when can they get it to us?"

"Friday," Dan said.

"Friday?" Ivy's voice broke on the word. "That's impossible. We need that bridge completed and ready for photos by Saturday afternoon."

"Yeah, I know, and I think we've got it covered," he said quickly. "If it's okay with you, I'm going to send a couple of the boys out to Tahoe to pick up the load and get it back here today."

"Of course it's okay with me." Ivy slumped against the counter as relief coursed through her in a thick wave. "You scared me to death, Dan."

He laughed. "Sorry, but since you're the boss I've got to run this stuff by you."

"Well, as your boss," she retorted, her voice teasing, "I'm ordering you to stop giving me heart palpitations. Or Angel Christmas Tree Farm is going to have to find a new manager."

"I'm not worried," Dan told her. "You can't fire a man who used to give you piggyback rides."

Ivy laughed at the memories he awakened. "Fine, fine. Get the guys on it right away though, okay? Will the crew be there to finish this up tomorrow?"

"You bet they will and they'll have that bridge built, sanded and painted by Thursday. I guarantee it."

"Thanks, Dan. Don't know what I'd do without you." She hung up, tucked her phone into her pocket and froze when Tanner's voice boomed out into the otherwise still room.

"You own Angel Christmas Tree Farm?"

Ten

She whipped around and her gaze locked with his. He was standing in the doorway, hands braced on the jambs, glaring at her as if he'd never seen her before. This was *not* how she'd planned for him to find out the truth.

"Oh, God. Tanner…"

"You are the owner of the Christmas tree lot."

It wasn't a question this time. It was a statement, said in a cold, hard voice, that sounded nothing like the man she'd come to know. This was going to be much harder than she'd thought it would be.

Hairy trotted past Tanner and went straight to Ivy. He sat down at her feet, looked up at her and whined a little as if in sympathy.

"Answer me."

"Yes," she said. One word and it couldn't possibly convey what she was feeling. Ivy's heart sank. She finally completely understood that old saying, as an icy hole opened up in the pit of her stomach and her heart dropped right into it. The look on Tanner's face chilled her to the bone.

She was so used to seeing a flash of humor in his eyes or even that shuttered look he got when he felt she was getting too close. The expression on his face now was one she'd never seen before. This wasn't hot fury, this was cold rage. His features were taut and his eyes were eerily blank as he gave her a look usually reserved for bugs under a microscope.

"You've been lying to me since the day you walked in here."

Stomach churning, eyes filling with tears she refused to shed, she nodded. "Yes. I have."

"Look at that," he mused in a sneer. "So you are at least *capable* of honesty."

That stung. Until he'd entered her life, she'd always been honest. "Damn it, Tanner. I didn't mean—"

"Please. Of course you did."

"Okay yes," she admitted, feeling a frantic rush inside to get out everything she wanted to say. "I did lie to you deliberately. I wanted to try to make you—"

"Horny? Well, congrats. It worked." He pushed off the doorjamb and folded his arms across his chest in a silent maneuver that told her plainly that he was already shutting her out.

"No," she argued. "That wasn't it."

"And I should believe you?"

This wasn't what she'd wanted, but maybe it was no more than she deserved. She had set out to trick him. To lie to him. To seduce him into not only liking her, but the town, the valley, so that he'd stop making trouble for her farm. She hadn't exactly gone into this with the best of motives. Was it any wonder that she was now getting kicked in the head by her own maneuvering?

"I only wanted to get to know you. To let you get to know me," she told him, words tumbling from her in a wild rush. "You were so determined to make trouble for the farm and you stayed locked up here so no one could talk to you, so—"

"Ah," he said, moving into the kitchen with a panther's deadly grace. Every move was quiet, contained and only defined the fury she felt pumping off of him in thick waves. "So your lies were *my* fault. You were forced to come into my house and lie to my face because I gave you no other choice."

Afternoon sunlight speared through the kitchen windows. The wall on the clock ticked so loudly, it echoed the heavy rhythm of Ivy's own heart. Hairy's whining crept up a notch in volume as if he sensed the tension mounting in the room.

She looked into Tanner's familiar eyes and

read only anger churning in those depths. Her heart ached and the cold that had a grip on her insides only deepened. She'd waited too long, Ivy told herself. She should have confessed all to him days ago.

"Tanner, you can at least listen to me," she said, never taking her gaze from his, despite how much it hurt to look at him and see nothing of the man she loved looking back at her.

"Why should I?" he countered, closing in on her. "You have more lies for me?"

"No." She sighed a little, then took a breath and said, "I was going to tell you today. I'd made up my mind that I couldn't pretend anymore."

"Yeah," he said dryly. "The strain must have been hard on you."

Through her misery, through the pain, her own temper started to flicker brightly. Yes, she had been wrong to lie to him. But she was apologizing, wasn't she? Standing here in front of him, letting him take potshots at her without firing back. Didn't that count for anything?

Oh, Ivy had been dreading this confrontation.

She'd known it was eventually coming. How could it not? He couldn't live in Cabot Valley and *not* find out the truth about who she was. But somehow, she'd hoped to find a better way of telling him than this.

Why hadn't she confessed all after their night together?

She knew why. Because she loved him. Because she had known even then that when the truth was finally out, she would lose this time with him.

Now she had to pay the price.

She lifted one hand to reach for him, then let it fall to her side, an unfulfilled wish. "It was. I hated lying to you. After that first day, I knew it was a mistake. But I couldn't find a way to tell you the truth, either."

"That's a lie, too, Ivy," he said quietly. "You didn't want to tell me. You were too busy trying to win me over."

"Okay yes," she admitted. "That was part of it. Sure. When Mitchell—"

His eyes went wide and a fast rush of color

filled his cheeks. "Mitchell? Damn it, I hadn't thought. Of course Mitchell was in this with you. He's the one who hired you! He *had* to know who you really were."

"Don't blame him," she said quickly, wishing she could pull her own words back. She hadn't meant to spill the beans on Tanner's friend and lawyer. That part had slipped out. "He called to talk to me about the complaints you'd been making and we started talking and things..." she threw her hands up in the air helplessly, "...just took off from there. I don't even remember whose idea it was originally."

"That's perfect," he muttered. "My best friend is in this with you. Both of you lying to me."

"You didn't give us much choice, Tanner," she snapped, feeling the growing edge of temper beginning to boil within.

He laughed. "So this is my fault?"

"No. I didn't say that," she said. "All I'm saying is that you don't make it easy, Tanner. You won't talk to people. You shut yourself away in this house and—"

"You've been here two weeks, Ivy. Every damn day for two weeks. You've had plenty of chances to talk to me. You just didn't."

"I knew going into this that I shouldn't lie to you, but I didn't know what else to do."

"Talk to me? Tell me the damn truth?"

"Oh, because you were so easy to have a conversation with," she retorted, feeling the sting of his accusation even as she admitted he wasn't that far wrong.

"You're really something," he said and his voice was low and tight. "You had me fooled. I really bought it all—hook, line and sinker. Have a good laugh every night when you went home, did you?"

"It wasn't like that," she insisted, wondering how she could salvage any of this.

"Then how was it?" His eyes narrowed on her as he chuckled darkly. "Must have panicked you when I showed up over at the farm."

"Yeah," she said. "It did."

"Now that I think back on it, you did look

more than surprised to see me. But I've gotta hand it to you. You recover fast."

Temper and misery were warring inside her and they were so tangled up now, she couldn't even separate them. His jaw was tight, his full mouth flattened into a grim line and his eyes were practically throwing off sparks.

"You took me on a tour," he said, with a slow shake of his head. "Introduced me to the owner, or who I thought was the owner…" He stopped, tipped his head to one side and waited for her to fill in the blank.

"My grandfather. Mike Angel."

"Right." He nodded. "So the family that lies together stays together?"

Okay, he could say what he wanted about her, maybe she deserved most of this. But her grandfather was off-limits. Mike had been against this from the beginning and damned if she was going to stand there and let Tanner King insult him.

"Pop had nothing to do with it," she told him. "He tried to stop me."

"But he didn't."

"No." His eyes were so dark now, Ivy couldn't even read the anger there anymore. He was locking himself away even as she stood there and watched him. Shutting her out. Shutting himself down. And there was nothing she could do to prevent it.

Seconds ticked past and the only sound was Hairy's tail thumping against the floor as if he were somehow trying to reach one or both of them.

"What about the sex, Ivy?" Those words were whispered, but the force behind them was clear enough. "All that a lie, too? You turn yourself into a martyr for the cause?"

Insulted now, she straightened up, lifted her chin and looked him dead in the eye. "No, it wasn't a lie. None of it was."

"And I should believe you because you're such an upright, honest person."

"You should believe me," she said, "because that was the most beautiful night of my life."

He tipped his head to one side and looked at

her as though he'd never seen her before. "I don't believe you. I think you were closing your eyes and thinking of England."

"*What?*"

"Old joke," he told her grimly. "And not funny."

"And not correct, either." This time, she did reach up to him but he jerked his head back before she could touch his face. "Tanner, I slept with you for one reason and one reason only."

He backed her up against the kitchen counter until she felt the icy edge of the granite against her spine. "What are you going to tell me now, Ivy? Truth? Or another lie?"

"I won't lie to you again, Tanner."

"Right."

He was waiting and he was looming and he was taking up every square inch of breathable air in the room. Her body was humming because of his closeness even while her stomach spun with nerves.

The temper building inside her was frothing, bubbling up through the thick layer of regret coating her stomach. Did he really believe she could have slept with him just to save her farm? Did he know her so little? Think so little of her? Yes, she'd lied, but that didn't mean she was a horrible person. For God's sake, they'd shared more than his bed. They'd spent time together, talked, laughed.

She'd fallen in love with him and all the while, he hadn't known her at all.

What a joke on her, Ivy thought. She'd lost her first love through an accident and now she'd lost the love of her life through her own damn fault. But maybe, she decided as she watched him watching her, they never would have stood a chance anyway. Because Tanner King didn't want to need anyone. And she needed to be needed.

She looked at him and knew it was over. Whatever they might have had was gone, blown away as completely as autumn leaves in a stiff winter wind.

There was no going back. There was no undoing what had been done. No more than she could unring a bell.

Since it was over, since she had nothing left to lose, she vowed that she would at least, leave on the truth. That much, she owed to herself.

"You know why I slept with you, Tanner?" she asked, keeping her gaze locked with his so he would read the truth of her words in her eyes. "Because I love you."

A long moment passed before he pushed up and away from her. "Oh, please. You expect me to believe that? You *love* me? How convenient."

She laughed now and the sound was harsh and brittle even to her own ears. "Convenient? Not even close." Ivy pushed one hand through her hair. "My God, do you think loving you is something I asked for? I've never met a more difficult man to love."

"Thanks very much."

She shook her head and walked to the kitchen table, where her purse was slung over the back of one of the chairs. Picking it up, she slid it onto her shoulder then turned to look at Tanner again.

"I'm sorry I lied to you Tanner. I really am. But mostly, I'm sorry *for* you."

He just stood there in a wash of golden sunlight, glaring at her as if she were an intruder. "I don't need your sympathy. I don't need anything from you."

"That's the really sad part," she told him. "You need so much. You need someone to love you. Someone to show you how to live outside the closed-in, sealed-off palace you've built here."

"And that's you, I suppose?"

"Could've been," she agreed, heart aching as she walked to the kitchen door. She turned the knob, then looked back at him over her shoulder. "I want you to remember that, Tanner. I would have loved you for the rest of my life." She gave him a tired smile. "But that's not your problem anymore. Oh, and one more thing. You don't have to fire me. I quit."

She walked outside, closed the door quietly

and left the man she loved and the future they might have had together behind her.

"You're fired."

Mitchell Tyler laughed into the phone and Tanner gripped the receiver so tightly, he was half surprised it didn't snap in half.

"Not funny, Mitchell," he snarled.

"Oh, please. You can't fire me."

"I just did."

Ivy had been gone for only a half hour and already, the silence in the house was beating at Tanner's brain like a hammer wrapped in silk. Every room echoed with her memory. He could still hear her voice in his mind. See her eyes at the last moment before she left, glistening with banked tears.

He could still feel the sharp stab of betrayal. So what better time to call the friend who'd set him up.

"You rotten, no-good..." Tanner muttered darkly.

"Tanner, what the hell is going on?"

"Ivy Holloway," he said. "Owner of Angel Christmas Tree Farm."

"Oh."

Tanner snatched the phone from his ear, gave it an astonished look, then slapped it back to his head again. "Oh? That's all you've got to say? You lied to me, damn it."

"Yeah, I did," Mitchell admitted freely.

Tanner grumbled under his breath and stalked a fast circle around the kitchen. Hairy was just behind him, his nails skittering on the polished wood floor. The chocolate cake Ivy had made still sat in the middle of the table, its scent wafting to him every time he got close. And even with all that had happened, even with the rush of anger still churning inside him, he couldn't help wishing that instead of chocolate, he could smell that flowery citrus scent of Ivy's.

Which made him the biggest damn fool in the world.

When he thought he could speak without shouting at his longtime friend, Tanner demanded, "Aren't you the guy who said you would always tell me the truth whether I wanted to hear or not?"

"I am."

"Then explain this to me."

Mitchell muttered something Tanner didn't quite catch and then said, "I tried to tell you what I thought before and you didn't want to hear it. You didn't leave me much choice."

He laughed a little at that. Both Ivy and Mitchell had somehow found a way to blame *him* for *their* lies. "How do you figure that?"

"Because you were being an ass, Tanner," Mitchell said flatly. "Calling the damn sheriff, threatening lawsuits every day when you called me incensed over a Christmas tree farm of all things. You were making yourself insane and aggravating the ulcer you already gave me."

True, he admitted silently. But the betrayal was still there. "I trusted you."

"And you still should."

He laughed shortly, without humor. "Why's that?"

"Because I'm your friend, Tanner," Mitchell

said on a heavy sigh. "We've known each other forever and I still have your back."

"You mean the one with the knife in it?"

"Jeez, you should have been an actor, not an artist," Mitchell muttered.

"And you should have told me who she was."

"You never would have let her in the house."

"Exactly," Tanner said. Then in the next moment, he realized all that he would have missed by not meeting Ivy Holloway. His mind dredged up dozens of images of her, one more haunting then the next. Ivy laughing. Ivy reaching for him. Ivy leaning over him, helping him solve the problems in the computer game. Ivy getting soaking wet while they bathed Hairy together.

Ivy.

Always Ivy.

"How'd you find out?" Mitchell asked after a long minute of silence.

Tanner stopped at the bay window in the kitchen and looked out the glass at the deepening twilight beyond. His gaze shifted unerringly to what he could see of the tree farm. The roofline of Ivy's house stood out as a darker shadow in the gloom. He pictured her there, alone, as he was. And he told himself that he shouldn't care where she was or what she did.

He'd trusted her and she'd lied to him.

Simple.

"I overheard her on the phone with her farm manager," he said. "When I confronted her, she told me everything. Threw you under the bus, too, though I don't think she meant to."

Mitchell chuckled. "I can take care of myself."

"Why'd you do it, Mitch?" Anger drained away now, leaving just bafflement. "Why'd you set me up? Why'd you help Ivy against me?"

"It wasn't against you, Tanner. It was *for* you. I love you like a brother, but you're shutting yourself off. Except for me and your brothers and cousins, you never see anyone anymore. You're closing yourself off, Tanner, and I don't like seeing it."

His friend's voice was serious, concerned. Tanner could admit, at least to himself, that maybe Mitch had a point. He *had* been more closed off in the last year or two than he used to be. He wasn't even sure why. It had been a slow-building thing, the pulling away from the world. He'd simply turned his back on…pretty much everything, he realized.

Hell, he hadn't been to visit any of his brothers in a couple of years. Hardly even spoke to them on the phone anymore, now that he thought about it. Working with Nathan on the game had been as close to sociable as Tanner had managed to get in longer than he cared to think about.

But that was his choice, wasn't it?

"And this was your answer?"

"Seemed like a good idea at the time."

Lights came on at the tree farm. Small white twinkling lights, strung between the telephone poles and wound through the branches of the trees separating the farm from his place. Had they always been there, Tanner wondered. Had he just never noticed them?

What else hadn't he noticed?

"Tanner, don't be so hard on Ivy."

He laughed and rubbed his eyes, trying to ease the headache pounding behind them. "Why shouldn't I be?"

"This whole thing was my idea, after all," Mitchell said softly. "Look, see it from Ivy's perspective. You were threatening her home, her livelihood. The King name carries a lot of weight in California. She knew that if you wanted to make real trouble for her or the valley that a judge would listen to you. Her life was on the line."

"Yeah, I guess…" He turned around, pulled out a kitchen chair and dropped into it. Reaching out one hand, he dragged a finger through the frosting on the cake and brought it to his mouth. Perfect. Of course.

"Besides, what did she really do that was so awful?" Mitchell asked. "She woke you up. Introduced you to your neighbors. Showed you how to *live*. So she had to lie to do it. If you'd known what she was up to, you never would have gone along with it, so cut her a break."

She had done all that. And more, Tanner thought, but didn't say. There were some things he wouldn't admit even to his closest friend. Things like what he'd been feeling for Ivy. Like the fact that his dreams were full of her. That his body hungered for hers. That since she walked out, he felt as though his heart had been ripped from his chest.

"Still want to fire me?"

"No," Tanner said and leaned back in his chair, kicking his legs out in front of him. "But if you come anywhere near me in the next couple of weeks, I'll kick your butt for you."

"Understood. And thanks for the warning."

When he hung up, Tanner realized that even though Mitchell had been part of the deception, that relationship was safe. He wouldn't turn from a years-long friendship even though Mitch had been part of the lie.

So why couldn't he forget what Ivy had done?

Because, he told himself, Ivy had betrayed him on a much deeper level.

She'd touched something in him that no one else ever had.

She had said she loved him.

And that lie he couldn't forgive.

Eleven

Ivy missed him.

Three days after she'd left his house, with angry words ringing in her ears, she ran her hand over the orange mesh walls of the bounce house and sighed at the images rushing through her mind. The first time Tanner had touched her. The first time she'd come apart in his arms. And the moment when she knew there would be more to come. How was she expected to forget about him, when his memory was all around her?

There were a couple dozen people wandering

around the farm at the moment. Families visiting their Christmas trees, others having lunch or shopping, and then there was her own crew putting the finishing touches on the setup for the wedding that was being held in the morning. There were at least a hundred things she should be doing. Instead, she was lost in her own thoughts.

She'd known it would be hard to be without Tanner. But she hadn't realized just how empty she would feel.

She had spent the last few days like a sleepwalker. She did her job, checked final arrangements for the big wedding that weekend and tried to pretend that everything was normal.

But it wasn't. And never would be again.

God, she thought, turning around to lean back against the inflated rubber castle, when David had died, she'd wanted to curl into a ball and cry for months. She'd thought her life was over and for a time, it had been. But she'd recovered, found her feet again and finally moved on.

Losing Tanner was so much more overwhelming. She hadn't lost him to death, she'd just lost him. He was right next door and might as well be as far from her as David. And this time, the pain was so huge that crying didn't help. Didn't ease the crushing pressure in her chest. She didn't want to cry, she wanted to fall into a hole and drag it in after her.

But once again, she couldn't give in to her own inner turmoil. There was even more at stake now than there had been four years ago. So she would keep walking. Keep working. And keep dreaming of what might have been.

God, she was an idiot. Why had she done it? Why had she started a relationship with a lie?

"Ivy?" From a distance, Carol Sands, the local florist, shouted to her.

"Yeah! Coming!" She dragged herself out of her thoughts and headed off to solve the latest crisis. No time to feel sorry for herself. That would have to wait until night, when she lay alone in her bed trying to sleep.

She joined Carol and fell into step beside

her, pitifully grateful for something to focus on besides herself and her own gloom.

"The bride's room is ready," Carol told her, a huge smile on her face. "I brought the flowers for the vase arrangements over now and stored them in the refrigerator. I'll bring the bouquets in the morning."

"That's good. The bride should be here by eleven." Ivy glanced at the people she passed and smiled at those she knew. Hopefully no one would notice that her smile wasn't exactly filled with warmth.

Carol was still talking. "Dan's got the umbrella tables set up in the meadow and the scarlet tablecloths Mrs. Miller stitched are at the gift shop in the back room."

"Right. We'll get everyone on it early tomorrow so it'll be perfect by the time the bride gets here." Bride. Wedding. Happily ever after. Well, she thought, at least *someone* was getting a happy ending. Her heart twisted in her chest, but she swallowed past the knot in her throat to say, "If you can be here by eight-thirty, we can get the centerpieces arranged and the crew will be here to help you out."

"That's great, thanks, Ivy." Carol grinned again and shoved her bright red hair back behind her ears. "This is a real shot for me, doing the flowers for a wedding this size."

"I know." This, she thought, was exactly the reason she had lied to Tanner. Why she had risked so much to try to reach him.

Since Angel Christmas Tree Farm was so far from any major city, the locals had quite a hand in helping with the event weddings. Carol's flower shop was growing by leaps and bounds. Mrs. Miller's alteration and tailoring took care of the tablecloths and any other sewing emergency. Bill Hansen's garden supply shop handled the tables, chairs and even the striped umbrellas that would shade wedding guests at the reception.

These events were helping an entire town to grow and thrive. Was it any wonder Ivy had been worried enough by Tanner's complaints to the sheriff to risk everything? Small consolation now though, she told herself. Had she saved her town only to doom herself?

They walked into the meadow and Ivy stopped to look around. The decorative bridge across the creek was perfect, just as Dan had promised. It gleamed snow white against the lush green background of the meadow grass and surrounding trees. It would be a perfect photo spot, she thought, letting her gaze slide across the hundred round tables that were scattered in a precisely laid out arc around the main table that was for the bridal party. Everything that could be done ahead of time was ready. The rest would wait for tomorrow.

She took a breath and let it slide slowly from her lungs. "I know how much this wedding means to all of us, Carol. So we've got to pull this off flawlessly."

"We will," her friend said.

Ivy hoped so. Because God knew, she'd given up a lot for this farm and a future that didn't look nearly as shiny as it had only two weeks ago.

* * *

Ivy was still walking his dog.

For three days he hadn't seen her, but the signs were plain enough. Hairy was exhausted and the leash was never where Tanner had last left it. So what kind of woman, he asked himself, proclaimed her love, walked out the door and then sneaked back in to visit a dog?

He pushed one hand through his hair and then scraped that hand across his face. His eyes felt gritty and he hadn't shaved in days.

He couldn't sleep. Couldn't work. Couldn't stop thinking about Ivy.

He'd told himself to forget about her. That she was a liar. Not to be trusted. That her claim of love was just another part of the game.

"But damn it, if that's true, then where the hell is she?" He glanced down at Hairy who looked up at him, as if trying to give his opinion.

Tanner stroked the dog's head and told himself that Ivy wasn't responding the way he'd expected her to. He'd seen this game played out far too often in his childhood to not know the moves.

She should be coming back to the house, trying to see him. Trying to convince him how much she loved him. She should have been there, trying to sway him, reel him in with tears and pledges of eternal devotion.

Scowling, he pushed out of the chair and walked to the back door. He threw it open and as he was slapped by a vicious wind, Hairy raced outside into the early night.

Moonlight spilled out of a clear, star-studded sky and painted the ground with shadows. The trees in the yard whipped and danced in a gale that had been growing steadily for the last hour.

He listened to Hairy's excited barks as the wind howled around him, but Tanner's thoughts were too busy churning to pay much attention.

"Why is she bothering to come and walk Hairy while at the same time she's deliberately avoiding running into me?"

He shook his head and tried to make sense of

it all. He didn't understand what she was thinking or what she was doing. If she wasn't trying to hook him, then why bother with the dog who loved her? None of this made sense.

He'd been waiting for her return since the moment Ivy had left. And now, he suddenly realized why. Because that's what his mother would have done. What his mother had done again and again in her all consuming quest for a fairy-tale ending she had never found.

His mother wouldn't have dreamed of announcing her love and then walking away. She had always found a way to stick around a man who didn't want her, trying to change his mind.

"Apparently," he mused aloud, "Ivy and my mother are two very different kinds of women."

Hairy's barking became more frantic and Tanner bolted from the porch to see what was wrong. The wind pushed at him, as if trying to shove him back into the house and he wondered where the hell the storm had come from. The sky was clear, but the wind was howling. Then, as quickly as it had kicked up, the wind was gone. As if it had never been.

Tanner finally reached the dog and it was then he heard what Hairy had. Voices. Shouting.

At Ivy's place.

Then he remembered the big wedding that Ivy was counting on to keep her farm safe was tomorrow. The windstorm had probably played havoc with all of her preparations.

Hairy barked again as if asking him what he was waiting for.

Tanner's brain shouted at him that this was the answer to all of his problems. If Ivy couldn't hold the wedding, she couldn't make the loan payment. If she couldn't do that, she'd lose the farm.

If that damn farm was gone, he'd have the peace and quiet that had once been so important to him. This was, in effect, the answer to everything.

Cursing under his breath, he sent Hairy back into the house.

* * *

Ivy was running through the meadow, shouting directions to the crew that had stayed late to make the final arrangements for the wedding.

"Good thing they stayed," she muttered under her breath as she looked around at the chaos created by the sudden wind blowing through.

Already, people were racing around under the soft shine of moonlight and the harsh glare of spotlights arranged around the meadow. Tables were turned over, neatly stacked umbrellas had taken flight and were lying every which way across the grass and into the trees. The delicate archway where the ceremony would be held was on its side and the ribbons streaming from it lay limp on the ground.

"Great," she said, reaching for the umbrella at her feet. It was heavy and cumbersome, but she managed and carried it to where the guys were already stacking the others they had gathered. "All that work and it's torn down in half an hour."

"We'll get it back up," Dan assured her. He

glanced at the clear sky spreading overhead and shrugged. "At least it's not raining."

"God, bite your tongue," she said quickly. "Have the guys set the tables back in their spots. With any luck, the wind's gone for good. We should be able to have most of this put back together before morning."

"On it," he answered and stalked off, shouting orders at a few of the men.

After that, Ivy just worked. She kept her head down and her mind blank as she busily set about fixing what Mother Nature had wrecked. As Dan had pointed out, it could have been worse, she consoled herself. If that wind had been accompanied by a summer storm, the meadow would be a sea of mud and they'd have had to come up with an alternate wedding site fast. As it was, this could be fixed and the bride and groom would never know anything had gone wrong.

Running across the meadow to join Carol in reattaching the bows to the arch, Ivy caught movement out of the corner of her eye. When she took a better look, she recognized Tanner, striding up the lane connecting the farm to the meadow. He stopped dead, met her gaze for a heart-stopping moment, then moved off without a word to join the men gathering up the fallen tables and chairs.

She took a deep breath as she watched him pitch in and help. She wondered what he was doing there, but couldn't afford the time to stop and ask him. A part of her wanted to believe that Tanner's being there might mean more than just a neighborly act. After all, when had he ever been neighborly? But at the same time, she remembered the distant expression on his face as they'd stared at each other, and she realized that whatever his reasons for being there—nothing between them had changed.

"What is it?" Carol asked, handing Ivy a length of white satin ribbon.

Her gaze fixed on Tanner until he was lost in the crowd of men working under the moonlight. Then she turned to her friend and forced a smile. "Nothing. It's nothing. Let's get this done, Carol."

Two hours later, Ivy was exhausted, but the crisis had been averted. Under the pale moon, the meadow lay lovely and perfect, as if it had never been disturbed. All was ready for the big event in the morning.

The dozen or so people who had worked so hard stood in a circle congratulating each other on a job well-done. They lifted cans of cold soda provided by Ivy in a toast to their efforts and laughed together over the night's activities. Tanner was on the periphery of the group and his gaze was locked on her.

His expression still unreadable to her, she watched as he took a long drink of the soda and then laughed at something one of the men said to him. If things were different, she thought sadly, she would walk up to Tanner and give him a big kiss as a thank you for all of his work tonight.

Instead, she was forced to remain quiet and still, uncomfortable under his steady regard.

When Dan spoke up, she was pathetically grateful for the interruption.

"Did you guys see King there, climbing that tree to get the umbrella down?"

"Hell yes," someone else said with a hoot of laughter. "Don't know how the damn thing got that high, but King scrambled up that old oak like a monkey."

Tanner smiled at the men and said, "Couldn't have been as funny as Tony falling off the bridge into the creek."

"Too true," Dan agreed.

Tony D'Amico grinned, despite his soaking wet clothes. "I thought I could lean far enough over the bridge to snag that damned thing. Turns out I couldn't."

"You were all great," Ivy said, speaking to them all, though her gaze fixed on Tanner alone. "I really appreciate everything you did, so I'd like to propose a toast."

Everyone lifted their cans of soda and waited. Tanner's gaze burned into hers and Ivy felt a rush of something hot and wicked pouring through her. Still, her voice was even and steady as she said, "To Angel Christmas Tree Farm and Cabot Valley. May this wedding be the boon we all need. And may we all remember tonight and what we accomplished…together."

"Together," everyone repeated and took a sip.

Tanner waited until the rest of them had drunk their toast before he lifted the canned drink in his hand toward her. *Together,* he thought solemnly. Tonight, he'd been a part of something. He'd belonged in a way he never had before. He'd worked with a group of people he never would have met if it hadn't been for Ivy and he'd helped them accomplish a task important to all of them.

It was an odd feeling for him.

And now it was over.

With his gaze locked on Ivy's, Tanner took a slow sip of the too sweet soda, then deliberately turned away. He couldn't look at her, awash in moonlight, without wanting to hold her, lose himself in her. But that time had passed. Now that the situation was resolved, there was no place for him here.

Still holding the can of soda, he walked down the dirt path that led to the front of the farm and the road to home.

The wedding was a huge success.

Not only for Angel Christmas Tree Farm, but for the town. The catering, flowers and decorations had all been wonderful. The guests who had driven out from San Francisco for the wedding had enjoyed themselves immensely and the bride and groom couldn't have been happier.

Still reeling from the number of people who had asked for her business cards at the event, Ivy sighed. Business would soon be booming, she knew. As soon as the article about the wedding hit the city newspapers, she knew Cabot Valley would experience the kind of success they'd all been dreaming of.

So why wasn't she happier?

She'd done it. Made a name for herself as an event destination. Salvaged disaster and created perfection. She'd seen to it that her hometown succeeded as well as she had and her plans for the future were brighter than ever before.

She should be blissful.

But then, how could she be really happy without the man she loved?

Without even the hope that they might one day straighten everything out? Yes, he'd come to her rescue and worked alongside her and her friends the night before the wedding, but since that night, she hadn't seen him. Not even a peek. Oh, she didn't expect to run into him in the early morning when she went to his house to take Hairy for a walk. After all, she went in the morning because she knew he'd be sleeping. But couldn't he have come by the farm again? Couldn't he have said something to her before he left that night?

"But then, what's left to say?" she asked herself glumly as she walked into the Cabot Valley bank. Her steps echoed on the polished linoleum and she sighed a little as she noted at least five people in line for one open teller. No quick trip for her this time.

She pushed thoughts of Tanner to the back of her mind to torture herself with later. For now, she had the final payment for the wedding in hand, and she wanted to pay off a big chunk of the loan she'd taken out to make all of this possible.

Ivy nearly groaned aloud when she spotted Eugenia Sparks in line. The woman was the biggest gossip in town and never had a kind word to say about anyone. The fact that Eugenia was even now talking to Rose Doherty in a voice that carried clear across the bank only irritated Ivy more because of the subject of Eugenia's venom.

"That Tanner King is a snob, if you ask me," Eugenia was saying, her voice carrying through the room to bounce off the high ceiling. "Too rich by half. Thinks he's too good for us is what," she continued with a sharp jerk of her head. "Imagine, the man's lived here in Cabot Valley for *months* and he never so much as shows his face at one town gathering. Thinks he's too good for us small-town folks. Not natural, if you ask me, a man staying to himself that way. Who knows what he's up to in that big fancy house of his."

Rose's eyes were glazed and Ivy thought she looked like a rabbit hypnotized by a snake, unable to look away.

Ivy, though, wasn't.

Spurred on by the emotions swirling inside her, Ivy forgot all about making her loan payment. Instead, she walked right up to Eugenia and looked her dead in the beady little eyes.

"Don't you talk about Tanner King that way," she said and had the pleasure of seeing the older woman's eyes widen and her mouth drop open in shock. But Ivy wasn't through. In her peripheral vision, she caught Rose's smile and encouraging nod, but Ivy would have continued anyway. "He's not a snob, either. Did you ever think that maybe he's lonely? That he doesn't know anyone in town?"

"Well..." Eugenia puffed up her chest and

tried to speak, but Ivy was on a roll and not to be denied.

"You say he's never been to one town function in the months he's lived here? Did anyone *invite* him? No." Furious and hurt on Tanner's behalf, Ivy defended him hotly and didn't have to ask herself why. She just kept talking. "Maybe it's not easy for someone to just show up unannounced when he doesn't know a soul. Maybe if someone had gone out of their way to invite him, he might have attended."

Eugenia huffed an outraged breath and narrowed her eyes as if for battle. Ivy met the woman glare for glare and refused to back down until her opponent did. Finally, Eugenia marched off to the teller when it was her turn and Ivy was left standing in line, practically vibrating with insult.

In the stunned silence of the bank, Ivy suddenly realized that she might as well have painted a sign over her head that read *Foolish Woman in Love*. Now, the town wouldn't be talking about Tanner, they'd be talking about her.

Fine, she thought as she turned and stalked out of the building. Better her than a man who couldn't defend himself against small town cats.

"I'm, er, sorry you had to hear that," the bank manager said in a low undertone. "But you shouldn't pay attention to what Eugenia Sparks has to say. No one does."

The man needn't have worried. Tanner hadn't given a good goddamn what the old woman with the sharp tongue had had to say. He'd been too busy watching Ivy and listening to her outraged voice as she defended him to her friends and neighbors.

He stood in the glass-walled office and looked out at the lobby without really seeing it. Ivy's words echoed over and over in his mind. He saw her eyes, glistening with tears she refused to let fall and he heard her voice, furious and hurt. And as he relived every moment of that little scene, the hard, icy shell around his heart cracked painfully.

He drew a deep breath and let it out again as his mind raced and his heart began to heal. He'd spent years hiding himself away, cutting himself off from anything that might connect him to another living soul. He'd been determined to protect himself from betrayal and yet, that was the biggest lie of all.

Living an insular existence wasn't really living. So what was the point?

The only question was, was it too late for him to change his life?

"Mr. King," the manager said softly, "is everything all right?"

He turned to look at the man in the crisp business suit. "Not yet. But if I have anything to say about it, it will be."

Ivy was still furious the following morning when she sneaked across Tanner's yard to collect Hairy for their walk. She never had gone back to the bank to make her loan payment, so

she'd have to do that as soon as she was finished here. But she couldn't ignore Hairy. She
knew darn well that Tanner would get involved
in his work and forget all about the little dog
that needed some exercise.

She walked up the porch steps and turned the
knob. The man never remembered to lock his
doors, so it was no problem to let herself in.
She quietly stepped inside and shrieked when
she saw Tanner standing in the kitchen, clearly
waiting for her.

She slapped one hand to the doorjamb to brace
herself and took a deep breath to ease the pounding of her heart. Hairy barked a greeting and
she leaned down to pet him even as she glared
up at Tanner. "Why do you keep scaring me?
Is it personal?"

He smiled. A gorgeous, make-his-eyes-sparkle
grin that made her knees wobble and did some
truly amazing things to the pit of her stomach.

"I've been waiting for you," he said.

"Yeah, I can see that," she told him and realized that he'd known all along that she was

coming here every morning to walk Hairy. "Why?"

"I have something for you." He pulled an envelope from the back pocket of his jeans and handed it over.

It was thick and white and had the logo of the local bank in the upper left hand corner. "What is this?"

"Open it and see."

She did and when she unfolded the sheaf of papers inside, her heart nearly stopped. It was the deed. To Angel Christmas Tree Farm. And across the top, in bright red ink was stamped Paid In Full.

Ivy swayed in place and instinctively shot out one hand to the jamb again, to help her maintain her balance. Stunned beyond words, she only stared up at Tanner in complete shock.

He was still smiling.

"Surprise," he said with a shrug. "The tree farm is yours, free and clear."

He looked so pleased with himself. Ivy shook her head, staring wide-eyed at him. It was the diamond watch all over again, she thought. He was still trying to buy her. To use his money to make an impact. And now he bought her *home?*

"You son of a bitch." Her voice was low and filled with the tears clogging her throat. "How could you do that?"

"What?" Confusion settled on his features but his eyes looked suddenly worried.

More furious than she'd ever been, Ivy couldn't believe that only yesterday she'd been defending him to the town. "I told you before, Tanner. I don't give a damn about your money. You can't buy me. Not with a watch. And not with a paid off loan."

"I'm not trying to—"

"Who gave you the right to stick your nose into my business?" she demanded and threw the loan papers at him. They hit him square in the chest, bounced off and landed unnoticed on the floor. "You don't own me. You never will."

She turned and sprinted down the steps and

across the yard. Ivy heard Hairy behind her, yipping excitedly as he chased her.

Tanner was just a step or two behind the dog. Damn it, he'd been up all night, waiting for her and trying to find the words he wanted to say to Ivy. But he hadn't come up with a thing. Instead, he'd just handed her the loan papers, hoping she'd understand.

Clearly, that was a mistake.

"Ivy, wait!"

She didn't even slow down, but his legs were longer than hers and desperation fueled his every step. He caught up with her at the base of an ancient oak tree. Hairy raced in delighted circles around them while Tanner grabbed her arm and spun her to face him.

"Let me go," she demanded as one tear tracked down her cheek.

That silent slide of sorrow punched Tanner dead in the chest. He'd brought this strong woman to tears and he wanted to kick himself for it. Which he would find a way to do. Later.

"Just listen, all right?" He blew out a frustrated

breath and stared down into pale blue eyes that haunted him every moment. "I've screwed this all up royally," he muttered. "I'm not trying to buy you, I'm trying to tell you I *love* you."

She went perfectly still in his arms and Tanner took a relieved breath. At least he had her attention.

Meeting his gaze with her tear-filled eyes, she asked quietly, "And do you always say *love* with your checkbook?"

He winced, then shook his head. "I've never said *love* at all," he admitted. "Maybe that's why I'm so bad at it. But I do love you, Ivy."

A brief smile curved her mouth and was gone again an instant later. Hope awakened and then died inside him just as quickly.

Irritated with himself, he released her and stalked off a few paces. "I don't even know how to say all of this. I've been awake all night trying to figure it out."

"You have?"

He glanced at her. "This is all your fault, you know."

"Really?"

"I heard the sarcasm there, but yeah, it is. You're the one who challenged me. Made me put my past behind me to look to the present and maybe even a future. You're the one who convinced me that Christmas isn't about misery, but about family."

She smiled again, but Tanner was too wound up to react to it. He felt as though he'd been waiting his whole life to get these words out and by damn, she was going to listen to him.

His gaze locked with hers across a distance of four or five feet. "You walked out on me, but you kept walking my dog."

"Yes," she said, voice soft and eyes shining.

He took a step toward her. "You're the one who wouldn't speak to me, but defended me in public."

"That's me," she agreed, her delectable mouth curving into a knowing smile.

He moved closer and his voice dropped, becoming a low throb of want and need. "You're the one who made me believe in happy endings, Ivy. You. It was always you."

"Tanner..." she sighed as he closed the last of the distance separating them.

"So now, you're just going to have to love me back," he said, "because I'm not going to let you go."

She lifted one hand to cover her mouth and made no attempt to stop the rush of tears coursing down her cheeks. Tanner pulled her into his arms and held her tightly, finally feeling his life slide into place. He kissed the top of her head and held on to her for both their sakes.

"Don't cry, Ivy," he whispered. "It kills me to see you cry. If you don't stop, I swear I'm going to go shopping for you again and then we'll have a big fight and—"

She lifted her head and stared up into his eyes. Laughing, she shook her head and said, "What could you possibly buy me, Tanner? You already gave me my *home*."

He used his thumbs to tenderly brush her tears from her cheeks as love settled into his heart and his soul, warming him thoroughly for the first time in his life. "The only thing I want to buy you is a ring, Ivy. One you'll wear forever."

"Oh, Tanner. Is that a proposal?"

"No, this is. Marry me, Ivy," he said, smiling. "Make me crazy for the rest of our lives."

She grinned up at him and threw her arms around his neck. Snuggling tightly to him, she said, "I love you so much, Tanner. Of course I'll marry you." She pulled her head back to look into his eyes as she gave him a stern warning. "But, you'll have to get used to working with noise because I want at least six kids and they'll all want to play in the Christmas tree fields."

"That sounds just right to me," he told her, resting his forehead on hers. "In the last few days, I discovered I can't work in the quiet any-more. An empty house is no way for a man to live."

"I guarantee you'll never be alone again, Tanner," she said, going up on her toes to meet his kiss.

In the early morning light, in the shade of an

oak, with a dog leaping against them excitedly, Tanner held his future securely in his arms.

And it was a deep summer Christmas.

Epilogue

It was the best wedding ever to be held at Angel Christmas Tree Farm.

The entire town of Cabot Valley had turned out to celebrate with one of their own.

Tanner stood to one side, with Hairy beside him, decked out in a brand-new collar with flowers threaded through it. The dog was humiliated, of course, but he—just like Tanner, would do anything for Ivy.

Watching his bride dance with the four-year-old son of the town florist, Carol, Tanner smiled. The little boy laughed with delight as Ivy spun in circles, moving to the rhythm of the music piped out on the overhead speakers.

"No Christmas carols," he mused, surprised to find he almost missed them.

"You look like a happy man," Nathan King said as he walked up to join him.

"I really am," Tanner said and felt the truth of those simple words slide into his heart. He'd never expected to find this kind of love and acceptance. He'd never hoped to be able to look into a woman's eyes and read her love for him written there. And he'd never known just how much love could change everything.

"She's a beauty," Nathan told him, lifting his bottle of beer in a toast.

"That she is," Travis King said, coming up on his cousin's other side.

All of the King cousins had attended the party and Tanner was grateful. Family was the constant of his life. And now he and Ivy would build their own branch of the King family dynasty.

"Rico's giving the bartender tips," Jesse said as he joined the others.

"Garrett's talking plants with Ivy's grandfather," Tanner told them. "Apparently, our cousin is thinking of expanding King Organics into public nurseries."

"With this family, there's always time for business," Travis said on a laugh.

"Not today, though," Mitchell said as he walked up and slapped Tanner on the back. "Today's the day my best friend gets to listen to me say *I told you so* for the first but certainly not the last time."

Tanner laughed and it felt good. Hell, if he had to listen to Mitchell gloat for the rest of his life, having Ivy would be worth it.

The music stopped then segued into another, slower song. On the improvised dance floor, Ivy set Carol's son down and turned to stare across the distance at her husband.

A slice of sunlight speared down from between thick white clouds to lay across Ivy like a blessing. She wore a strapless white dress that belled into a wide skirt. Her long hair was hanging loose in tumbled curls and a wreath of yellow roses encircled her head while lemon-colored ribbons trailed down her back.

He left his cousins behind as he walked to the only woman he would ever love. "Hello, Mrs. King."

"Dance with me?"

"Always," she said, moving into him and locking her gaze on his.

Taking her in his arms, he swept her into a dance that had everyone else clearing the floor to watch. But there were oblivious to their guests. It was as if the two of them were alone in a private, romantic world of promises and new beginnings.

"You are the most beautiful woman I've ever seen," he whispered.

"Don't look now, Mr. King, but you're talking like a man in love," she said softly.

"I am indeed," he said and lowered his head to hers. As they kissed, a cheer rose up from the surrounding crowd and Hairy barked his approval.

* * * * *